The Easter Bunny that Ate My Sister

Also by Dean Marney:

The Turkey that Ate My Father

The Jack-O'-Lantern that Ate My Brother

The Christmas Tree that Ate My Mother

Dirty Socks Don't Win Games

The Computer that Ate My Brother

The Trouble with Jake's Double

You, Me, and Gracie Makes Three

The Easter Bunny that Ate My Sister

Dean Marney

AN **APPLE** PAPERBACK

SCHOLASTIC INC.
New York Toronto London Auckland Sydney

ISBN 0-590-69335-2

Copyright © 1996 by Dean Marney. APPLE PAPERBACKS and the APPLE PAPERBACKS logo are registered trademarks of Scholastic Inc. All rights reserved. Published by Scholastic Inc.

12 11 10 9 8 7 6 5 4 3 2 1   6 7 8 9/9 0 1/0

Printed in the U.S.A.   40

First Scholastic printing, March 1996

For Dylan

The EASTER BUNNY that Ate My Sister

1

He made me sign it. *He* is my stupid little brother, Booger. Yes, we all know some people call him Booker. They are wrong. His real name is Booger, or "Boog" for short.

He had this piece of paper that he was waving in my face like it was something special.

"Stop it," I spit at him, "I'm not signing anything."

"You have to sign, or I'm telling," Booker whined.

"Tell what?" I asked.

"Tell the whole story to the whole world including your friends and all the people at school and Mom and Dad," he said. "They'll know you're crazy."

"Who cares?" I said, but I still sort of did. "No one will believe you."

"They'll have to believe me," he said with confidence. "I have proof. I have the rabbit."

Electric spider legs went up my spine.

"Give it here."

"No way," he said. "Only if you sign. You get it only if you admit to the world I saved your life."

"It's my rabbit," I said.

"It's mine. You didn't want it." He smirked.

It was a good point — but one I wasn't willing to give in to.

"You'll give me the stupid rabbit if I sign?" I asked, driving my eyes into his teeny tiny brain to see if he was lying.

"Absolutely," he answered.

"Are you lying? Let me see your fingers. I want to make sure nothing is crossed."

"I don't lie," chirped Booger.

"Right," I said. "If you were Pinocchio your nose would be the size of Florida."

"Very funny," he said. "Sign or you'll never see the rabbit again."

"Exactly," I said.

I jerked the piece of paper out of his dirty little hand. If you threw grass seed and water on his hands I swear he could be a Chia Pet. I read the piece of paper. " 'I, Lizzie, admit that my wonderful brother, Booker, saved me. In return for one stuffed bunny, I promise to give him the respect he deserves and will call him by his real name.' "

There was a line on the bottom for me to sign and date the document.

"You have to be kidding." I quizzed him. "Don't

2

you think respect is asking a bit much? How about a simple 'thank you'?"

"Respect," he said.

I stared him down. "I want to see the bunny first," I demanded.

He went to his room, slamming his door so I wouldn't be able to see where he'd hidden it. In a little while he came running back with the bunny.

"Here it is," he said, holding it tightly against his body.

"Where did you find it?"

"It doesn't matter," Booger replied calmly.

"I can't believe you kept it," I said, staring at the rabbit.

"Why not?" he stupidly asked.

"After what it put me through?" I said, raising my voice.

"It's just a dumb stuffed bunny now," he said.

"Ya, that's what you think," I said. "Hand it over. You don't know what you're doing."

"Sign," he said.

Ya, it may have *looked* like a normal stuffed bunny. It had shrunk back to normal size. It even looked a little cute.

Don't they all look cute and cuddly? I think they pride themselves on looking cute. It's a trick. The ribbon on this one was now twisted and the fur seemed a little worn in places. Now, I noticed that one eye was looser than the other. The pink of its fur was different, too. It looked faded and uneven.

I thought about wrestling it away from Booger, but then I'd have to touch him. I took the paper over to my desk and signed it. I came back across the room and waved it at him.

"Give me the bunny," I said.

"No, give me the paper first," he said, looking at me suspiciously.

"At the same time . . . agreed?" I said slowly.

"All right," he agreed.

I extended my arm with the paper and he extended his with the bunny. With our other arms we grabbed for what we wanted and each other had. We played a little tug-of-war for a minute with both of us trying to hang on to both the paper and the bunny. Finally, we looked at each other in the eye just to freeze frame the moment and, with a final tussle, gave up. When we stood back, Booger had the paper and I had the bunny.

Booger looked down at the paper. He was re-reading it. It took forever. His lips were moving, too.

He screamed.

"Stop screaming," I yelled.

"You tricked me. Give it back." He was still screaming.

"I didn't trick you," I said.

"You're a liar," he yelled.

"I am not. I just made a small change in one

sentence," I said, quite pleased with my inventiveness.

Instead of reading "the respect he deserves," I inserted "the *lack of* respect he deserves and will call him by his real name — Booger."

"You should have checked it . . . before," I said. "You should be grateful I'm teaching you a lesson."

"You cheat," he yelled and stormed out of my room, slamming his body into everything. "I saved your life," he continued to mumble down the hall, tearing up the piece of paper as he went, and letting the pieces drop on the floor.

"You're picking that up," I said.

He turned and looked at me with this awful hurt look on his face like I'd just sold his baseball card collection, which I almost did once. I don't know why he got all upset over it. I was going to get a good price and I was even going to split it with him, sixty/forty.

"I saved your life," he said. "I deserve respect."

"Yes you did," I admitted, "but it isn't like I've never saved yours."

He was pounding his fat little feet down the stairs. For a second I felt a weensy little bit of guilt. I set the bunny down on my bed and ran out of my room and over to the edge of the stairway.

"I'm sorry, Booker," I said sincerely. It was

double sincere. It was triple sincere. It was so sincere, I could have been on a witness stand.

"For what?" he yelled back at me.

"For . . . I don't know."

I started to say, "For not being a good sister and thanks for saving my life," but I couldn't because I was struck dumb.

I couldn't move or talk. All I could do was listen to the sound of light thumps coming from my room. Yes, I'd heard this sound before. It was the soft, muffled sound of a stuffed bunny moving across the floor.

2

It all started with my two worries. Well, I have lots of worries, but I have two really big worries. I don't want to be crazy and I don't want to be killed.

My mother says, "How can someone your age worry about such things?"

I ask, "How can you keep from worrying about these things?"

I'm not sure when I started going crazy. My name is Lizzie and I'm not really the crazy type. Some people may argue, but that's my honest opinion.

Crazy things happen to me, but that doesn't make you the crazy type, does it? It could be hereditary. There are crazy people all over my family.

About a month ago I woke up afraid. It wasn't a little afraid. It was big afraid. It was total and complete terror at the thought of getting out of bed.

I was suddenly afraid of everything that was going on in the world. I was afraid of being abducted, killed, mutilated, run over by a drunk driver, and anything else including the sun burning out, a crazy person coming into our school and shooting all the kids, someone putting poison in all the breakfast cereal, or the hole in the ozone getting big enough so that the whole world burns up.

People might think I had a simple case of fearing death. Well no kidding. Like do you want to be killed? I didn't think so.

Really, I'm not just afraid of dying. I know everyone has to die sometime. I'm afraid of being killed. There's a huge difference.

Before, I used to wake up and not really think about anything except maybe about what I was going to wear to school or what homework I hadn't finished the night before. Now, I would wake up too scared to roll over. I started thinking everyone was trying to get me and I'd better watch it. I didn't feel safe anymore.

I'd say to myself, "Lizzie, do you realize every day you wake up it's another chance for someone to get you?"

I went downstairs.

"Good God, what's the matter with you?" asked my mother.

I told her. "I woke up afraid of everything."

"That's interesting. Like what?"

I gave her the short list.

"Well, honey," she said, "those things are not going to happen to you."

"How do you know?"

My dad put down his paper and looked at me like I really *was* crazy. I didn't like it one bit.

"You're afraid of all those things?" he said.

I was afraid if they started thinking I was crazy and that maybe then they'd have to lock me up and put me away and I'd never see anyone again. I'd have to live in a place with bars on the windows and wear my pajamas all day and play badminton. I hate badminton. Finally another crazy person would dress up and pretend to be a nurse and try to kill me.

I decided I'd better cool it.

"Just kidding." I smiled.

"No, honey," said my mom. "If you're that worried we should talk about it."

"No, I'm fine," I said.

"I think," my dad reasoned, "that you need to stop watching TV. You've probably just seen ten too many horror movies."

"Like that would help?" I wanted to say.

I didn't know why I was worried and afraid. What good did knowing why do you? I knew why. It just wasn't safe anymore.

My parents quickly decided that it was just a phase. My mother had a concerned look like it was probably all her fault because she made me buy school lunch instead of making one for me like other mothers do, but I could tell she liked the idea that maybe it *was* a phase.

"Everybody does that," she said like she knew; "you'll grow out of it."

I didn't exactly grow right out of it that minute. I just learned to live with it. I held on every day, being afraid, trying to be normal, and being extra careful not to show it so they wouldn't think I was crazy. Then this whole bunny thing started.

The bunny thing began a week before I got out of school for spring break. It happened to be the week before Easter. My fears just started hopping — I mean popping out.

That Saturday I'd gone to the grocery store with my dad. I was sure we were going to be killed by a trucker falling asleep at the wheel, and if we made it, a terrorist was going to blow up the grocery store.

My dad is so bizarre. He acted like the world was a safe place. He was berserk. He talked to every stranger in the store. He sang to the store music in the produce section. He even danced down the cereal aisle. He's the one that is nuts.

I'm not totally one hundred percent sure, but I'm almost sure that my dad has been an alien abductee. I'm scared they'll come after me, too. They do that. They go through complete families.

I read about it in a magazine while we were waiting in line at the grocery store. The first thing the article pointed out is that people who have been abducted don't act normal. That's my dad . . . well, and my mom and Booger, but that's something else.

My dad is just especially weird, and when we got home and we were unpacking the groceries, I tried to tell him why. He wasn't the least bit interested. I told him he had memory lapses, which the article said victims had. He told me he didn't.

"What about the time you lost the car keys?" I said. He looked at me, puzzled. "See, you don't even remember forgetting."

"Your mother had them," he answered.

"You still forgot," I said.

"Lizzie," he demanded, "I am not and have never been an alien abductee."

"You're just in denial, Dad. The article I read said most abductees are deep in denial. You just don't remember it yet because the whole experience was too frightening."

"Lizzie, this is going beyond irritating. Quit. Quit now," he scolded. "I'm going in-line skating. You want to go?"

"See," I said, "you're into fitness, another sign, and you're a vegetarian. Do you notice that in-line kind of sounds like alien?"

"Lizzie," he said sort of patiently, "I have high blood pressure from conversations like this. I want to have lower blood pressure. That's why

11

I work out and stay away from eating animals. I want to live long and have you drive me crazy in my old age."

"Denial," I sighed, "big denial. Guess what?"

"No," said my dad.

"Booker was probably an alien baby. Look at his beady eyes."

"Way too far, Lizzie. Find something to do. You're jumping headfirst here into being in major trouble. Leave your little brother alone. You have five days, and then you are out of school for a week for spring break. Try to hold it together until then."

"Dad," I said. I was a little irritated myself. "I'm just trying to help."

Booger came into the room.

"Where's Mom?" he mumbled.

"Talk clear," I said.

"I wasn't talking to you," he said, squinting his little beady alien eyes at me.

Dad answered, "She's somewhere working on her thesis."

In case you don't know, a thesis is like a super-big paper that my mom has to write to finish school — for now that is. She loves school even though she is going crazy writing her thesis and she's making us crazier.

"Oh," said Booger, "I was wondering when we were going to decorate for Easter."

This would push my mother over the edge. She

can't stand extra messes right now. She said she doesn't have time for them. And then Booger would get in trouble for asking. I loved it.

When you decorate for Easter there is extra mess. The first thing you do is get out that fake plastic grass stuff and it gets all over the house and our vacuum cleaner won't pick it up. My mom really loves it.

"Not yet," my dad said. "Can't we wait till we dye some eggs?"

"You're going to let us dye eggs?" I asked, surprised.

"As long as I don't have to eat them," he said.

I wasn't even thinking about eating them. No one eats them at our house except you-know-who. That's why I didn't think we'd dye any this year. I also distinctly remember my mother saying we were never dyeing eggs again after last year when Booger made me spill a cup of red dye on the kitchen floor.

"I'll eat them," said Booger.

"How can you eat something that smells like that?" I asked him.

"Like what?" Booger answered.

"Like a you-know-what. Like hard-boiled eggs. They're disgusting."

"Lizzie," my dad interrupted. "Stop."

"You're the vegetarian," I said.

"I don't care," he said.

He turned to Booger. "We'll dye eggs at the

13

end of the week. Probably Saturday. Maybe we'll decorate tomorrow after we go to church."

"If you eat them," I added, "you can get salmonella poisoning and die."

"Cannot," said Booger.

"Can too," I answered.

"Stop," said my dad.

"What is salmon poisoning?" Booger asked my dad.

"It's salmonella, a bacteria that can get on food that is improperly handled, cooked, or stored," my dad explained. "You're not going to get it."

Booger seemed satisfied. He's so stupid.

"I think we need some new decorations," said Booger, moving right along.

Suddenly I got a piercing pain in my head, like a ski pole was being pushed through my ears. My breathing went all funny. I winced.

"Liz," said my dad, "what is wrong with you?"

I closed my eyes and as suddenly as the pain hit, it left.

"Maybe I'm an abductee and they left something in my brain," I blurted to my dad. "I'm serious."

"I don't think so," was my dad's response. "I think you had too much sugar today and you need some exercise."

"What were we talking about?" I asked.

"New Easter decorations," Booger said.

It happened again. When Booger said Easter

decorations, I got that pain again. I realized a possibility. It could be a sign. It could be a big sign.

If it was a sign, the question was, did the sign mean we needed new decorations or I had a brain tumor? That's the trouble with signs, you can't always tell what they mean. You can be totally wrong and get into a whole bunch of trouble.

I tried to think about it reasonably for a minute, telling myself that it also could be that it wasn't a sign or a serious health condition. I told myself I could be getting a tension headache or I had developed an allergy to Booger's voice. Then I thought some more. If Booger wanted new decorations, then the truth was, we probably shouldn't have them.

"We don't need them," I said.

"What did you have in mind, Booker?" my dad said with his mouth while the rest of his face was telling me to shut up.

"I think we should do bunnies in a big way this year," said Booger.

The pain again.

"Lots of bunnies," he went on, "big and little and all sorts of colors of bunnies."

My head was killing me.

"That's ridiculous!" I screamed.

"Lizzie," Dad said calmly, "nice overreaction. Booker, we'll see. If it's convenient, maybe we'll get something new."

"Okay," chirped Booger.

He is so irritatingly perky.

"I have to go lie down," I said. "I don't feel well. I'm probably dying from some killer virus."

3

We didn't decorate Sunday after church, which, by the way, was, well, a little too churchy. It was long and too boring except for a couple of things. The only real fun part was that it was Palm Sunday, so we all got these pieces of palm leaves that actually look like swords and we used them to tickle each other on the neck.

Palm Sunday is the start of Holy Week, which ends in Easter. Palm Sunday is when Jesus rode on a donkey into Jerusalem before they crucified him. People cheered at him like he was a king and laid palm branches down in front of him, which is what, I guess, they did for kings. Anyway, that's why we get palms on Palm Sunday. It's a tradition. My mother says it doesn't have to make sense if it's a tradition.

When you get tickled with palm leaves, it feels like you have a bug on your neck. I did it to my mom. She didn't think it was funny. She jumped about sixty-three feet. I thought she was going

17

to have a heart attack right there in church.

That has happened. Not to my mom, but it happened to this other guy. Once, right during the sermon, they had to call the ambulance to come in and get this guy who was lying down on the floor. It was scary.

We sat there very quietly while they put him on a stretcher and took him to the hospital. That was a Sunday everyone stayed awake.

Anyway, my mom grabbed my palm sword and bent the crap out of it and put it in her purse. I tried to steal Booger's but he was being a brat about it. My mother pinched my leg really hard and I almost screamed but I knew I'd be in worse trouble if I made any sound at all.

Sometimes I do really well in church. Then sometimes it is really hard to sit still when everyone is saying "Sit still." I guess it is because everything around you is so quiet and you can't stand it and you just have to move.

This is the really weird thing that happened that Sunday. I was sitting there trying real hard not to fidget. If I move my legs back and forth and up and down real fast, it makes the pew squeak and drives my mother crazy. To take my mind off the fact that my whole body was going to sleep and I needed to move bad, I started looking at the lady in front of me that had this big mole on her neck. I was wondering if she shouldn't probably get it removed because it was most likely a rare form of cancer and it was probably going to eat a hole through her body.

Then out of the corner of my eye I saw something start to move. It was small and looked fuzzy. It was on the floor up front by the altar.

I shifted in my seat to see it better. It darted. At first I thought it was a huge rat. That would've been something.

It wasn't. It was a bunny, which was still something. A rabbit was in church and running.

The whole episode took only about ten seconds. He or she was there, then ran, and was gone. I loooked around to see what everyone was going to do. I figured this was going to be as good as the guy with the heart attack.

No one was doing anything. They were all acting like nothing happened. They were acting like it happened all the time.

I elbowed Booger.

"Did you see that?" I whispered.

"Knock it off," he whispered back.

My mother said, "Shhhhh."

"Did you see the bunny?" I whispered softer.

"What bunny?" said Booger.

My mother gave us both a dirty look.

I was ticked. Here was a major event, and everyone was just ignoring it. How often do rabbits come to church?

I waited till a hymn and asked my dad if he saw the rabbit.

"Is this a riddle?" he asked me.

"No," I said.

"Sing," commanded my father.

We went up for Communion and I looked for rabbit droppings. Rabbits always leave droppings. We had a rabbit in kindergarten and every time we let it out of its cage, it left droppings everywhere. Our teacher went insane making sure we didn't touch them or pick them up. Like anyone is that stupid, besides Booger.

I couldn't see any. I looked pretty carefully, too. I considered the slight possibility that maybe I imagined the whole thing, but I didn't think so.

In the car on the way home I asked everyone, "Was there a bunny in church or was it just me?"

"Just you," said my dad. "I didn't see any other rabbits."

I wanted to remind him that he was an alien abductee so he better not be making fun of me, but I thought better of it.

"Sorry Liz, just kidding," added my dad. "Where and when did you see a bunny in church?"

"Up front," I told him. "It ran in front of the altar right during the middle of church."

"Lizzie," said my mom, "that's ridiculous."

"None of you saw it?" I almost pleaded. "I'm not making it up."

"Nope," said my dad.

"I didn't," said Booger.

"Lizzie, that's silly," said my mom.

"Really?" I asked them.

They looked at me like I was really really crazy.

I sort of laughed like it was no big deal or that maybe I was just playing a joke. All the while I was thinking about that mental institution and homicidal maniacs dressed up like nurses.

Then I had the thought that maybe they were playing a joke on me. It was probably a plot to make me think I was going crazy. Then I thought maybe everyone saw it and decided to pretend that they didn't see it and forgot to tell me.

I took a huge deep breath. I was thinking nutty and I knew it. I knew that it was a crazy idea so I felt okay because then I also knew I wasn't crazy. I heard on a TV show how if you think you're crazy, you're not. It's when you think you aren't crazy that you probably are.

I wasn't going to give them the satisfaction of knowing it mattered to me. I told myself it was just one of those things. It was one of those days when you see a rabbit in church and no one else does. It didn't mean the rabbit wasn't there. It just means you saw it and no one else did.

I shut up about it, but questions kept coming up in my brain. I couldn't stop thinking them. What was a rabbit doing there, and where did the rabbit go? Was there like a rabbit town under the church? Was the church built over an ancient bunny burial ground? Was it now being haunted by bunnies?

Booger broke my concentration.

"Are we going to decorate for Easter today?" he asked.

My mother groaned. I knew she was thinking of that fake grass stuff all over the house. She was obsessed with Easter grass. She needed professional help in my opinion.

"Do we have to?" she asked him back.

Booger said, "Yes."

Typically, she listened to him, sort of.

"Honey, let's do it on Wednesday after school. I have to do some schoolwork this afternoon and I don't want to dig for the box with the Easter decorations in it today. I'll find it this week while you're in school."

"Okay," said Booger.

"I don't care if we decorate or not," I said. "It's not like it's Christmas and we're going to get presents or something."

Now I ask you, was that a horrible thing to say?

My mother explained, "Lizzie, we don't have to always be materialistic. We can do things just because they give us pleasure."

She said it like I'd just said we should kill all people with blue eyes.

"What does that mean?" I asked.

"That means," said my mom, "that we don't do

everything just because you get a reward. There is lots of value in doing some things just because you do them for the sheer joy of it."

"Okay," I said, but I still didn't get what I said that was so wrong. "Whatever."

4

It was Monday morning and I was getting a little excited about spring vacation. It isn't like we were going to do anything or go anywhere. My dad had to work and my mother had school. What looked good to me was not having to go to school or do homework for a week.

I was actually glad we weren't traveling. The thought of a car or plane wreck didn't exactly thrill me. I knew it had to be safer at home.

Speaking of school, we had to do another project that we had to present to the entire class. I swear that is all we ever do. I don't get it. The worst thing was we had to do it by the end of the week, before spring break.

My dad says it's good because public speaking is like almost everyone's number-one fear, and this would be good practice in overcoming it. As you know, I could think of a ton of things I'm more afraid of — like drowning in quicksand or being bitten by rabid bats or finding a poisonous snake in my sleeping bag or falling down an elevator shaft, and I hoped that we weren't going to practice those.

This project could be anything we wanted to present to the class on spring. I thought that covered a lot of territory. We could talk about plants or animals or read a poem or paint a picture or anything, as long as it had to do with spring.

Mrs. Rose, our teacher, said, "Go ahead, think of something a little wild and springy. Have fun with it. Express yourself uniquely. Surprise yourself. Write a song. Make up a play. Do a dance."

Since I'm still kind of into Greek mythology, I thought I'd tell the story of Persephone and Demeter. I like it, but it can be very scary if you think about it. Well, guess what? We had to write down the subject matter of our projects on a list. Probably to make sure no one was doing something totally inappropriate like Scott would.

I checked over the list. I couldn't believe it. The odds were probably better that I'd win the lottery. Weird Janelle was doing the same subject, the same myth thing, except she was doing a ballet to it. Wouldn't you know. She's totally weird and I knew I'd have to change my subject.

Mrs. Rose called us both up to her desk.

She said, "So you're both doing the same myth. I've got a great idea. Why don't you do it together? First, though, tell me what you were each planning on doing."

Janelle said, "I'm doing an impressionistic ballet to symbolically tell the story."

She is so weird. I didn't even know what that meant but it sounded strange. She's really stuck-up, too. She thinks she is so smart. She thinks I'm really dumb. We're not best friends.

I went to a slumber party once, which I don't do anymore because I read where some psychopath abducted a girl from a slumber party. The last one I went to was at Amy's house and Janelle was there because Amy's mom made her invite her because Amy's mom was friends with Janelle's mom. Janelle was a total loser. She had to stretch her legs all through the movie we were watching and she complained because the movie was too violent and she wanted to watch opera or something.

She would suddenly throw her legs straight up in the air during the scariest parts and then shoot them sideways, knocking things off tables and hitting people in the head so no one could even see the screen. I think she just had to remind us all the time that she was taking ballet. I wasn't impressed. I wanted to remind her I had taken self-defense and was going to karate chop her if she didn't stop.

When we were going to call up some boys and then hang up, she said, "I don't think we should." No one likes her.

"Won't that be exciting," beamed the teacher.

She turned to me, "And Lizzie, what are you going to do?"

"I was just going to tell the story, you know, just kind of tell the story the way I read it."

I could see her disappointment.

I tried to be more creative. I added, "I could show some pictures out of the book."

"I know," the teacher said, all enthusiastic, "wouldn't it be better to work together? Janelle, would it work if Lizzie told the story and you acted it out through dance? Do you think that has creative possibilities?"

I prayed, No, please say no.

"Well, maybe," Janelle pondered. "I can sort of see it working. It might be fun."

"What do you think, Lizzie?" asked the teacher.

"Uhhhhhhh," I said, sounding extra intelligent. I wanted to tell her I thought it would be ridiculous. I didn't want to be with a geek who was going to dance around the room and everyone was going to freak out and laugh at us.

"Perfect," said the teacher. "If I give you time to work on it today, could you do it tomorrow?"

I was in shock.

"Sure," said Janelle.

I was trapped.

"Uhhhhhh," I said again.

I couldn't believe it. This always happened to me. It seemed like in every class, whenever we paired up, I got the weirdest person in the class.

We practiced. I mean, Janelle practiced. I tried to hide. She had to warm up first by doing the splits all over the place. It hurt just to watch her.

She said, "I don't want to pull anything by not being properly warmed up."

I wanted to tell her she was going to pull her pants apart if she did that again, but I didn't.

"You know," she said, "I was going to perform this to music, but since you're going to be telling the story, I'll just let you be my music." She beamed me a big perfect-toothed grin. Her dad is a dentist.

I wanted to say, "Don't smile at me. This has disaster written all over it."

She then asked me what I was going to wear.

"I think," she said before I could answer, "we should dress like the ancient Greeks."

"Sorry," I said, "all my ancient Greek clothes are at the cleaners."

She laughed but she didn't mean it.

"Well," she sighed, "let's give this a try."

We were in the corner of the room and everyone was supposed to be working on their presentations. I could see they were all kind of glancing at us. It was a bad sign.

I started telling the story. It isn't that complicated. There's a mother, Demeter, who was the goddess of agriculture. Demeter had a daughter, Kore, which means maiden, who later changed her name to Persephone.

Anyway, Demeter and Persephone are like real close, unlike some mothers and daughters. One day, Persephone was out in the meadow and because Cupid had put an arrow through Pluto's heart (Pluto was the underworld god), Pluto fell in love with her. At first I could only picture Pluto as the Disney cartoon character. Later I pictured him much scarier.

Instead of asking her out on a date or something, he abducted Persephone in his chariot and took her underground to be his bride. Word has it she wasn't exactly thrilled by the prospect of living in the underworld with all the dead people. Well, no kidding, how much fun could that be?

Her mother, Demeter, didn't know what happened. She just knew Persephone wasn't around. She was so upset that she went all over the world looking for her daughter. My mother probably would have thrown a party instead. Finally a flaky river nymph told her what had happened and that Persephone was now the Queen of the Dead. Queen of the Dead sounds like a great horror movie, doesn't it?

Well, Demeter was beside-herself nuts. She went to Zeus, who was king of the gods, and begged him to do something. Zeus said he'd get her back on one condition, that Persephone hadn't eaten anything in the underworld. Well, no kidding, fat chance, a girl has to eat sometime. Excuse her, she made a mistake of getting hungry and ate a pomegranate.

A compromise had to be reached because of the stupid pomegranate. Persephone would live with Pluto half the year and her mother half the year. The time of year that she was underground, Demeter stopped things from growing so you had fall and winter, and then when Persephone came aboveground, Demeter was happy so there was spring and summer.

Picture me trying to tell this story with weird Janelle jumping and looking stupid all over the place. She also needed to put on some more deodorant, if you know what I mean.

"Do you think I should wear my toe shoes?" asked Janelle.

"I'm trying to tell the story," I said.

"Sorry," she said, "I was just trying to make it better."

I could see Scott and his friends laughing at us. I knew this was going to be a total disaster. I tried not to look at him or Janelle.

I was losing my place in the story.

"I'm keeping my movements small today," said Janelle. "They'll be much bigger tomorrow."

They looked plenty big to me.

"Where am I supposed to stand?" I asked.

"To the side," she replied.

I wished she had said "outside," and I questioned again, why was this happening to me?

5

I don't mind being a little weird. In fact, I think it's kind of cool to be slightly weird. However, I do mind being *totally* weird with the whole world making fun of you and thinking you might be crazy.

I admitted to my mother a long time ago that I was afraid of being too weird. I was really asking her if she thought I was crazy.

"You're not adding a new fear to your list, are you?" she attacked me.

I answered, "Well . . . no . . . sort of."

It was the wrong answer. I don't know what the right one was. She said I had to just stop being afraid of everything all the time — like I wouldn't do that if I could. She said I was afraid of being weird because I was just afraid of criticism. Right, like anyone likes to be criticized. She didn't help me at all.

School was finally over for one of the worst Mondays I've had in a long time. I was complain-

31

ing to Bob, my best friend — yes, she's a girl and Bob is her name.

"Do you think I'm totally weird?" I asked her.

"No," she said. "You're weird, but it's good weird."

I started ragging to her about how I always got stuck with the weirdest kid in the class to do things with.

Bob told me to lighten up.

She said, "Why take it so seriously? It's a dumb presentation. No one cares."

"I'm in front of the class," I said. "I just hate making a fool of myself." I paused and then added, "Which is why I do it all the time."

"You said it." Bob laughed.

Changing the subject, I said, "Do you realize we haven't had a fire drill in months? What are we supposed to do if we have a real disaster around here?"

Bob acted like she didn't hear me. She was getting used to me being worried and afraid of everything. She also just got her braces and that's all she can think about. She's, like, one of the first people in our class to get them. They are driving her bananas. She got both her uppers and her lowers at the same time. She said she can't even look at candy or gum or her braces will break.

She's always carrying a toothbrush around with her, which is both a little gross and weird. She's obsessed with not being caught with food in her braces. I told *her* to lighten up.

We were waiting for our buses to go home. I was eagle-eyed, watching out for any strangers that might be trying to grab someone. I was furious because my parents had never given us a secret code word. As we were standing there, Janelle came flying at me with her arms waving like she was a crazy homicidal maniac.

"Elizabeth!" she screeched. "Elizabeth!"

"Ya, what?" I asked impatiently.

"I'll call you at home so we can talk about tomorrow."

"You don't need to do that," I said.

She didn't hear me. She was leaping over everything and everyone to get to her bus, which was already pulling out.

"Wait!" she screamed at the bus driver.

"She's a little strange," said Bob.

"Yup," I said, "and she's my partner. Big deal, right?"

"You got it," said Bob. "Do I have food in my teeth?"

"No way," I said. "You haven't eaten anything and you've brushed your teeth fifty thousand times."

I said good-bye to Bob and got on my bus. I hugged her because I didn't know if this would be our last time to see each other. I heard on the news last night that a bus in the Middle East had a suicide bomber on it. Booger asked if I wanted to sit by him

"What do you think?" I said.

I sat in the back. At one point we had to go over some railroad tracks. The bus stops and the driver opens the door, which I always think is pretty funny. Like if there is a train coming, it will just go through the door and out the window?

When the bus stopped I happened to look out the window. From where I was sitting I could see the railroad crossing sign.

"That's strange," I said, but no one heard me because they were all talking and it was totally noisy.

The railroad crossing sign that usually had railroad tracks and a big "X" on it now had the silhouette of a bunny and a big "X." It was a bunny crossing sign. Don't you think that was a little strange?

We got home and the minute I walked through the door my mother said frantically, "Who is Janelle? She's called you four times in the last five minutes."

"Mom," I sighed, "she's very weird and we're doing a presentation together tomorrow and she's going to make me look like an idiot."

"Well," she said, calmer, "that's nice, dear. Maybe you're overreacting — again. She seemed more enthusiastic than weird to me."

"Mom, one word, 'nuts.' That covers it. She's going to dance in front of the class tomorrow wearing something from ancient Greece."

My mom almost leaked a small look of surprise.

"Really?" she said. "What are you doing?"

I wanted to really shock her and say "I'm going to wear a dress and stand on my head," but of course I didn't. I'm not nuts — remember?

So I told her, "I'm telling the story of Demeter and Persephone and she's dancing the story."

"Oh," my mom said, slightly relieved, "that sounds quite unusual. No wonder she's excited."

"Mom," I repeated, "she's nuts."

"Elizabeth, keep a good attitude," she said, wagging her finger at me.

I hate it when she does that.

"Okay, I will," I said, making my voice as deadpan as I could get it.

"There're some bunnies on the counter and yogurt in the fridge for a snack," she said.

"Did you say bunnies?" I said frantically.

"Hardly," she said. "I said bananas and yogurt."

"Oh," I said, sticking my fingers in my ears to make sure nothing was in there.

"Please, wash your hands with soap before you eat anything," she added.

She didn't have to worry about me. I read an article where it said just by washing your hands several times a day and especially before you eat, you can cut the number of colds you get to practically zero, let alone all the diseases we haven't even heard of yet. I went into the kitchen.

Booger was sitting at the counter watching the little TV, which he isn't supposed to do. To make it worse, he was sitting there with his finger up his nose. I didn't think he noticed me come in.

I snuck around behind him and went, "Boo!" I did it actually to be nice. I was giving him practice in dealing with terrorist attacks. He should've thanked me.

He jumped a mile and rammed his finger in his nose, which I actually hadn't planned on him doing. I honestly didn't scare him that much. Anyway, he got a teeny little bloody nose because he shouldn't have had his finger in there, and I had to go to my room. I was grounded again.

At the end of my life someone will ask me what I remember and I will truthfully answer, "I was grounded a lot."

The good thing was when Janelle called again, my mother told her I was grounded and couldn't come to the phone. The bad thing was that I was looking out the window at the time and I swear I saw something I shouldn't have. I saw a pink bunny hop across our yard. It was big. I mean big. Bigger than any bunny I'd seen. It was as big as a German shepherd.

It was pink and it looked up at me. It knew I was watching. I don't mind telling you, it gave me the creeps. It hopped into the neighbors' backyard and then who knows where. I got underneath my covers with my clothes and shoes on. I kept thinking what the headlines would be — innocent but crazy girl abducted by giant pink bunny aliens.

6

On the way to school Tuesday I was thinking that maybe Janelle was also an alien abductee. I thought that maybe she was even an alien herself. I figured she was probably an alien and she was going to abduct our whole class.

The night before, I dreamed Janelle and I switched places. Janelle was telling the story and I was dancing. I had on a long, ugly, mud-stained wedding dress and I didn't know any steps. I didn't know what to do.

She was speaking in a foreign language and my dress was too long and heavy and it seemed like it was getting heavier. I was trying to pretend that I knew what I was doing but I couldn't move very easily. The dress was getting heavier and finally it was so heavy I couldn't move at all. I just stood there, now up on top of a ladder, which I didn't know how I got on. I was frozen, unable to move at all, as the entire class sat and laughed at me.

All day the presentation was bugging me. I just didn't want to do it. It was dumb.

Janelle kept bugging me about it, too. I was trying not to make it a big deal and she kept driving me crazy about it. She sent me a note that we should eat lunch together to talk about it.

I race-walked and almost got in trouble so I could be at the front of the lunch line. Then I bolted my lunch down before Janelle could even pick hers up. I then spent the remainder of my lunch break hiding from her in the library with Bob, who, as a true friend, only left my side to go and brush her teeth twice.

I was glad we weren't first. Jeff was first. He's like a Mr. Science. He was going to show us how to figure out the date when Easter would fall during any year. He lost me in two seconds flat.

He started telling us that Easter was always the Sunday right after the full moon that occurs after March 21. I was asleep. Then he put a chart on the wall with letters and numbers and he said if you had the right number and the appropriate letter you could find Easter Sunday in the year 2099.

I wasn't going to argue with him. I don't think anyone followed what he was saying. No one asked any questions, not even the teacher. Maybe he should have danced it.

I glanced around the room to see if anyone else was awake, and I noticed something. Janelle was missing. She had just been there. I had no idea where she went. Jeff was finished.

"Thank you, Jeff," said the teacher. "Lizzie, are you and Janelle ready?"

"I don't know where Janelle is," I said timidly.

"I'm here," sang Janelle from the back of the room. She had changed her clothes and was on the floor warming up.

She stood up. She did not look like any ancient Greek I'd ever seen. She looked like she had on her mother's old blue nightgown over her pink leotard and tights. She had on her pink toe shoes.

"Is that what you're wearing?" I asked as we cleared a space for her to dance.

"Yes." She beamed. "Isn't it perfect?"

I wanted to say no but I said, "Perfect."

She instructed me to go to the far side of the room to stand, which sounded good to me. I would have been more thrilled if she had said for me to go out into the hall.

"Talk loud," she whispered.

Janelle took five or six giant ballet duck steps and stood, facing the class, in her mother's blue nightgown. She was in the middle of the area we cleared and she proceeded to wrap her arms and legs all around herself. It looked like yoga. I wondered if this was one of the bigger movements she talked about yesterday. She held the position like a statue. I was amazed.

Mrs. Rose nodded at me to start. Stupidly, I

looked at Scott, who was already laughing, and in order not to laugh myself, I focused my eyes out the window. I shouldn't have. I went crazy and thought I was going to throw up.

Moving across the playground, I saw a pink ghost bunny. We're talking six feet tall and transparent and filmy, like it was there but it wasn't. I could see it clearly only when the sun was hitting it right. It had seen me and it was looking right at me.

"Oh no," I whispered, "it's happening again."

"Elizabeth?" asked the teacher. "Did you say something?"

"No, I mean yes, I mean . . . " I answered.

"You can start," she said impatiently.

"Sorry, oh yeah." I got a grip on myself.

I started the story but something was different. Either it was the story or the bunny, or I was totally flipping out. All of a sudden I couldn't see or hear the class around me. It was like I was there but I wasn't. I could hear myself telling the story but it was like it was someone else.

I felt like I was outside everything. Talk about not feeling like yourself. How about not feeling yourself period. As I listened to myself tell the story, I could see I really was outside, in the country somewhere, and instead of seeing Janelle, I could see Persephone. I just knew it was her.

I could see her playing in the sun and then I saw the ground move like waves on the water.

The ground split and Pluto burst out of it in his chariot pulled by the blackest, meanest-looking horses you've ever seen. They were big and wild-looking and their massive muscles bulged, strained, and rippled.

The horses weren't the only thing with huge muscles. Pluto had muscles bigger than anything I'd ever seen. His arm muscles were flexed and all tense as they held the reins of the horses. We're talking buff beyond belief. It looked like the horses were shooting fire and smoke out their nostrils.

Then Pluto was chasing Persephone. At first, it seemed like she didn't know what was happening. Then the horses and chariot were coming after her like they were going to mow her down. She started running. She didn't have a chance. There was no way she could get away. Then Pluto just swooped up Persephone like a sack of brown rice and took her in his chariot down below the earth. To say I was terrified for her is to put it mildly.

Then I saw her mother looking for Persephone and crying. She was thinking Persephone was dead and thinking she was going to die, too, because she'd lost her daughter. I wanted to cry with her.

"Don't worry," I yelled across the field to her. "She's a queen now. She'll be okay. She'll come back."

I finished the story and the room came back into

focus. I looked at Janelle, who was doing the splits with her arms in the air. I looked at the class, expecting them to be laughing hysterically.

They weren't. They were silent, with their mouths hanging open like baby birds waiting for food. I brushed water away from my eyes. Had I been crying?

Mrs. Rose was clapping and smiling. "Girls, girls, that was beautiful. It was simply wonderful." She came up and drew us together and hugged us both at the same time.

Janelle took a huge ballerina bow and everyone clapped some more. I just stood there. I felt weird beyond belief. I glanced out the window. I half expected to see Persephone out on the baseball diamond but instead I saw the pink ghost rabbit smiling. Then a breeze went through it and it was gone.

What was even stranger is that I looked at Janelle and I didn't think she was a geek anymore. I had the craziest thought: I wanted her to be my friend. I think I needed to lie down.

7

I really don't know what happened. Everyone kept telling me that it was great and that Janelle was weird but not too weird. They thought I was something special. It made me a little nervous.

Even Scott said, "That was cool."

For a minute, I was feeling pretty good. I felt a little bad that I hadn't actually been there to see and enjoy our presentation, but what the heck. I almost forgot about being afraid — almost.

I went home on the bus determined to keep my good mood. I walked into our house. Booger, of course, had beat me home.

"Hi," I said to my mom.

"Hi," she said back. "How was school?"

"Okay," I said.

She didn't ask me about the presentation. She'd forgotten all about it. She moved right on to talking to Booger about something.

I could have said something. I could've reminded her and told her about how great it was, minus the part about the pink bunny rabbit. I didn't though. I felt sorry for myself. I felt like she didn't care.

It was ugly. Why did I do it? I was feeling so good before. I let myself feel bad because she forgot and then I just jumped into that feeling and swam around in it.

I went upstairs and lay on my bed feeling every ounce of sorry for myself I could dig up and drag out. The phone rang. A jolt of fear shot through me. I had been feeling miserable, now I was miserable and afraid.

My mother yelled up, "Lizzie, it's for you. It's Janelle."

I went to the phone even though I didn't want to because it was probably an obscene phone caller who had told my mother it was Janelle to trick me.

"Hi?" I said, tentatively trying to sound like someone else besides myself just in case.

"Hi," said Janelle. "Elizabeth?"

"Ya, it's me," I said in my normal voice.

"Did you think it was okay?" she asked.

"Ya," I said, still bummed.

"Do you think I was too much? You know sometimes I get so into it that I forget about what other people think. It's really stupid and gets me into all sorts of trouble," said Janelle, laughing.

"No," I said, "you were just fine. It was great."

"You were just inspiring," she gushed. "You were so passionate!"

"Well . . . " I said, pleased with myself.

Janelle said, "Oh, I have to go now. I have to go to ballet class. Do you think you'd like to come over sometime?"

"Sure," I answered.

I got off the phone and my mom was right beside me.

"Lizzie," she said in the rush of one breath, "I almost forgot. How did your dance go?"

I felt slightly better that she at least remembered me. She did care about me.

"It really went well," I said, like it wasn't a big deal at all. "It surprised me. No one laughed."

"Isn't that just terrific?" she said, all happy for me like I'd just won a giant contest or something.

You know I wanted to hug her, but I didn't. I wonder why? I almost hate growing up. Half the time I do things I don't want to do and the other half I don't do things that I really want to do. Somebody figure it out, please.

"Lizzie," she added, "we have to go shopping. You don't have a thing to wear for Easter. Maybe I could pick you up after school and we could see if we could find you a new dress."

"Okay."

"Why don't you go outside before dinner and get some fresh air?" my mom suggested.

I considered the possibilities. I wanted to go

biking. It seemed reasonably safe. You can always make a quick getaway unless you get a flat tire.

I grabbed my helmet to make sure I didn't get a major head injury. I grabbed a bicycle-tire repair kit my dad had gotten for me, although I didn't know how to use it, and put it in my pack with my water bottle and a flashlight, in case there was like an unexpected eclipse and it got dark.

I also took my safety whistle, which is like major loud and I'm only supposed to use it in an extreme emergency. I thought I was ready. Oh, I also put a recent picture of myself on the hallway table so if I didn't show up they could show the police my picture immediately.

I mustered up all my courage and went out to ride my bike until dinner. Booger was at a friend's house. Even though I was afraid, I was out riding by myself and that felt kind of good.

It was sunny and warm enough not to need a sweatshirt, but I kept mine on. I was doing "the loop." It's a route with not very much traffic that we ride on. My dad has figured it's about three miles.

I was just riding, minding my own business, when about one hundred feet in front of me I saw a small white animal with markings on it. I got a little closer and I could see it was a bunny. It was moving about twelve to fifteen feet ahead of me down the road.

I sped up, trying to catch up to it. I shifted

gears and pedaled faster. I caught up with it, it stopped, and I slammed on my brakes.

I was right there beside it. It was a real bunny rabbit and what I thought were markings was a cute little navy blue jacket. It was a dressed-up bunny. It stopped, turned, and gave me the once-over.

Get this, and I'm telling you the truth, not only was it dressed but it had what looked like a small basket in its front paws. It inspected me for a few seconds. I almost thought it was going to say something. It didn't. Instead it turned and hopped into the bushes.

I'd swear to you that I just saw the Easter Bunny. I didn't know *what* was going on. I know I saw a bunny dressed like an Easter Bunny and I was starting to freak out just a teeny little bit. I knew for absolute sure I had to be crazy.

I didn't complete the loop. I turned my bike around and rode like a speed demon home.

"I just saw another bunny and this one was the Easter stupid Bunny!" I screamed without thinking while entering our back door.

Standing in the kitchen was my mother's best friend, Judy.

"Elizabeth," said my mother. "What are you talking about?"

"Uhhhh," I said, totally embarrassed.

"Yes?" my mom asked.

"The Easter stupid Bunny?" asked Judy, laughing.

"Well," I explained. "I saw this rabbit that I thought just had dark markings, but then I got up close and I think it was a coat and it was carrying a basket."

"The coat was carrying a basket?" asked Judy. "That's some coat."

"Really Elizabeth," said my mom, trying to make me not look nuts. "You have such an imagination."

I was showing my secret again. I was walnuts and they knew it. I was trying not to do that. I started doubting my ability to see and act and think. I told myself to keep my stupid mouth shut. I wondered if, when I grew up, I'd push a shopping cart around the neighborhood and mumble about the Easter Bunny.

"Just kidding." I tried to laugh.

Booger came into the room. He was home and the little creep had been listening.

"The Easter Bunny doesn't come till Easter," he said.

"You moron," I said, "there is no such thing as the Easter Bunny."

"I know that," he snapped.

I bet he didn't. He's so dumb.

"Elizabeth," said my mother tightly, "Judy is here and she doesn't need to listen to us fighting about the Easter Bunny, now does she?"

"It's okay," said Judy, "I have to go. I have to get home and listen to my kids fight. You guys are making me homesick." She rapped on my bike helmet, which I'd forgotten to take off.

I exited the room quickly before Judy left so I could try to miss the lecture my mom would give me. She's got this thing about me not fighting with Booger in front of company. Judy was gone.

"Elizabeth," yelled my mom, "I need to talk to you."

I could hear Booger bugging her. "When are we going to decorate?"

8

It was a full moon. It woke me up. Before I realized it was the moon, the first thing I thought was that it was morning. It was like a giant headlight and it was shining right in my eyes.

I flashed on Jeff's presentation, you know, the incredibly hard and boring math problem on how to find the date of Easter. Well, he said Easter was the first Sunday after the full moon after March something. He was right, and see, I did learn something in school.

Something inside me made me get up and go to the window. I mean, I could've just rolled over and gone back to sleep. I didn't.

I went to the window and stared right up at the moon. It was so clear I could see the seas and the big craters. It seems weird that they call areas of the moon seas like there is water up there. I guess when they called them that maybe they thought there *was* water up there?

I wondered why they thought there was a man in the moon. To me, the moon looks much more like a beautiful woman. She's all silvery and soft and quiet.

My window was open. My mom must have opened it. She wanted me to get kidnapped. I could smell spring. It smelled like dirt and something sweet, too.

I could feel the cool night air on my face. It felt good. Then I realized it was dead quiet out. It was eerie. Nothing was moving. There wasn't even a breeze.

The moonlight was reflected by the shiny new leaves already on the tree next to the house. I thought how moonlight makes everything look soft. Things don't have hard edges or distinct shadows by moonlight. Things kind of run together. They're smudged.

I let go and relaxed a minute. I thought, I like spring. Then I quickly came to my senses and looked down into our yard to make sure no one was down there.

"Look," I said to myself, "isn't that pretty? Talk about soft, the yard looks like it is covered with snow in the moonlight."

Then I had a complete panic attack and a scream got caught in my throat. The snow was moving. The snow was an animal. In fact it was more than one animal, it was lots of them.

I stepped back from the window. I didn't want

them to see me. Then it hit me that I knew what those animals were.

Barely out loud I whispered, "Bunnies."

Our front lawn was covered in bunnies. There were mostly white bunnies, but there were some spotted ones and some brown ones mixed in. There were probably even some black ones, but bunnies they were.

I had to tell someone. What if they ate the house? What if they were killer bunnies? I was going to go get my dad up.

Then I saw something else. There was something coming down the road. I thought it was a large dog.

"Oh, oh," I said.

It wasn't a dog. It was too large. Even at a distance, I could tell it had a huge snout, a humongous tail, large ears, and big teeth that reflected the moonlight. I thought, The better to eat you, my dear.

I was positive it was a wolf. It had to be a wolf. No dog looked that much like a wolf. I hate to admit it but I even thought it could be a werewolf. Wasn't it a full moon?

The weirdest thing and the scariest was its eyes. They were greenish yellow. They lit the area in front of the werewolf like flashlights.

I thought at least some of the bunnies were done for. They were about to become wolfie snacks.

"Run, hop, whatever, just do something." I

wanted to yell at them, but I didn't want the were-wolf to hear me.

The wolf stopped and sort of crouched like it was trying not to be seen. That was highly unlikely because it was so large. Then, in unison, all the bunnies stood up and looked straight at the wolf. They were frozen statues staring at him, and so was I. I couldn't move. It was like I was hypnotized.

Then this cloud moved in front of the moon. It was a weird kind of cloud. It was the only one in the sky and it was black and thick. It got really dark. I couldn't see the bunnies or the wolf. Everything was still silent, but the smell was different. It smelled even more like dirt. It smelled like wet dirt from a deep hole.

"Move, cloud!" I said out loud, breaking the silence and forgetting I was afraid.

On my command it moved, and as it did the bunnies and the wolf just vanished. I mean they literally disappeared. I guess it wasn't instantaneous but it was fast. They became kind of a fog that drifted up above the house and then floated deep into the night sky.

I told myself I was dreaming but I knew I wasn't, but I guess my other choice was that I was you know what — crazy.

"What is this bunny thing?" I asked myself. "Why won't they leave me alone?"

I slammed the window shut and locked it tight.

I got into bed. Then I got back up and changed my nightgown so I could prove to myself in the morning that I hadn't been dreaming. I also wrote myself a note.

It said, "Dear Elizabeth, You aren't dreaming. There were bunnies on your lawn — lots of them and a werewolf, too. Love, Lizzie."

Okay, it was dumb, I know. I was only a little tired. It was at least something.

The next morning my mother yelled up that I was going to be late for school.

"You'll need to hustle," said my mom.

I looked at my nightgown and it was the second one I put on last night. My first one was on the floor right where I left it. I then did a Janelle leap over to my desk. There was my note, which made me feel good.

That is, except for one little thing. There was an added note. It wasn't in my handwriting.

Underneath what I wrote, it said in tiny little print: THINGS DON'T ALWAYS MAKE SENSE.

My legs felt like they were going to collapse under me. I felt hot and then freezing. I had beads of sweat on my forehead.

I was extremely scared. Someone had been in my room and they were telling me that things don't make sense. I tell you what doesn't make sense. I could've been abducted.

I screamed. Now *that* made sense.

55

9

Do you know what it is like to have bunnies on the brain? Do people die from going crazy? It was now Thursday and I decided I would put bunnies completely out of my thoughts. It didn't work. You try it. For one minute I want you to think about anything but bunnies. Go ahead, try it.

Well of course, you can't help but think about bunnies. I'd tell myself not to think about bunnies and realize that I was still thinking about bunnies by trying not to think about them. I was ready to scream.

I never wanted to see a rabbit again and they were everywhere. I'd never realized how many bunnies there were. Especially in the newspaper — since it was so close to Easter, they were on every page. They were on TV. They were on my cereal box. There was even a bunny on my night-gown. I couldn't get away from them.

I never wanted to see a rabbit again. I wasn't

ever even going to eat a chocolate one. I was grateful my parents didn't cook bunnies for dinner. At Bob's house they do.

"It's okay," says Bob. "You don't think about it and it tastes just like chicken."

"Exactly," I answer. "Then why not just eat chicken?"

"I don't know," says Bob.

With two days to go till we got out for a week, school was pretty high energy. We were starting to wear out our teachers and you could tell. It wasn't on purpose, either. Well, for some of the kids it was on purpose.

It was mostly the boys who were in trouble. Matt and Juan were both getting it for being smart mouths. They practically got the whole class kicked out of music. If you get sent back from your music classroom to your regular classroom, you might as well kiss it all good-bye. You are in major trouble.

Jess should have been in trouble for being a dumb mouth. He was saying "I don't know" to everything just to drive everyone berserk. It started on the morning bus ride and he did it all day. He thought it was the most hysterical thing that had ever been done.

Louise said, "Is that all you're going to say?"

Jess replied, "I don't know."

I'm telling you, it really gets on your nerves. I wanted to ask him if he wanted me to punch him in the gut and see if he said, "I don't know," and then I'd punch him and ask him if he knew now. I didn't, however, because there is too much violence in the world and I don't want to add to it — although punching Jess shouldn't count as real violence.

However, we're doing peer mediation. Our school is trying hard to eliminate all violence and make our school completely safe. I think that's a real good thing. But it doesn't work. The counselor, who is a total dweeb, picks his little pets and supposedly trains them to solve problems. If you get mad at someone you're supposed to go to one of these people, called a peer mediator, and each of you tells your side of the story and then you work out a solution that makes everyone happy. Wrong! The people who have done it so far are still mad at each other, plus they now both hate the mediator.

I think it would probably work better if they let everyone get trained as a mediator instead of just the pets. Then there wouldn't be anyone left to fight. We'd all be too busy mediating. Of course no one asked my opinion.

I didn't see any bunnies in the morning. I didn't see any at lunch. I did have kind of a bunny lunch. I ate carrot and celery sticks, but I do that a lot so it wasn't that strange. Our lunchroom supervisor kind of looks like a rabbit with glasses but that doesn't count either.

The afternoon was looking good. It was bunnyless. We had P.E., and Sara and Jessica were the team captains. Sara doesn't like me on account of I accidentally nudged her just slightly in the lunchroom in first grade and she dropped her tray and spilled vegetable soup on her favorite shirt. She says she will never forgive me.

She was picking all the popular people and Jessica wants Sara to like her so she was picking the people she knew Sara wouldn't want. Since Sara doesn't like me, Jessica picked me and so I was on the unpopular team. Well, the joke was on them, we were playing soccer and we beat them bad. When it comes to soccer, popular doesn't mean a thing.

Of course we had Janelle on our team, who, of course, is not popular. Usually she is too out to lunch to be of, like, any help on a team, but now since we're friends, I was like coaching her. Well, I'm here to tell you that the girl can kick. She still kind of dances around, which is sort of irritating, and you have to kind of remind her which team she's on now and then, but other than that, she was a real asset.

We didn't end up having Jessica, our team captain, on our team. We were captainless and we still beat them. She got hit in the face with the ball in the first two minutes of play and spent the rest of the period lying down with ice on her face.

My mom was picking me up after school to go

look for an Easter dress. I knew it was worthless going. I knew she knew it, too. We both knew that it was worthless going, but we were going anyway.

I suppose it is one of those things you have to do. There is no choice. Daughters have to go shopping for dresses with their mothers.

I knew she would pick out things I wouldn't be caught dead in, and everything that I liked she would absolutely hate.

She'd say, "Oh Lizzie, no," in this tone of voice like I'm a complete idiot, or she'd say, "That's too much money for a dress."

Call me psychic if you want, but I knew we were going shopping and the chances of me buying a dress were not too great. I knew we'd argue, I'd come close to crying, and then I'd end up wearing last year's dress, which she picked out and I also hate and it's too tight in the arms and there will probably be a drive-by shooting at the mall. I've done this all before.

When it was time to go, our teacher stood at the door and shook our hands as we exited. It's something new. It's supposed to teach us respect or something.

It's okay. I kind of like it except I think she should make people wash their hands first. It seems like an awfully good way to pass killer *Ebola* germs.

I'm not as bad a germ freak as my mother. She

turns into a Tasmanian devil if she has to use a dirty rest room. I hold it if the bathroom is dirty. I simply don't use them unless I absolutely have to super bad.

My mother says, "People are pigs, just pigs."

It ruins her day, I'm telling you. Sometimes she takes rubber gloves out of her purse and cleans the rest room. I swear to you, and it is the most embarrassing thing you've ever seen. What's worse is she gets complete strangers to help her and they will all be in there cleaning away, talking about people being "pigs, just pigs."

We shook hands and then the teacher told us, "Good-bye. Have a great vacation. Read a book or two, even. I won't see you tomorrow. You'll have a substitute."

"Who?" we groaned together.

"Please," she said, "I do not know who the substitute will be but I'm sure you will show him or her the proper respect and conduct yourselves responsibly and in a way that I know you are capable."

Right, we all thought as we looked at each other.

I left the school building, and it felt great to be outside again. I really do like spring. It was warm and I was in a fantastic mood. I only glanced around briefly to make sure there were no snipers. I felt mildly safe and good.

That is, until I got to the car. Booger was already in the front seat. He had the window rolled all the way down.

"It's my turn for the front," I said.

"No it's not," said Booger.

"Yes it is," I said, trying to open the door, which he had locked.

"Get in the car please," my mother said through clenched teeth.

That was it. I was now in a totally bad mood. I got in the backseat and lay down.

"Elizabeth," snapped my mother, "sit up and put your seat belt on."

I sat up. I put my seat belt on. I lay back down.

"Elizabeth, you're not making this enjoyable," said my mother, kind of singing it.

"I'm preparing myself in case we have an accident," I said, and then I sang back, "I should be sitting in the front seat."

She didn't sing back, which was a good thing because otherwise I'd be living in an opera.

Opera (we learned this in music) is a play where they sing all their lines. I missed it on a test so I had to learn it and retake the whole stupid thing. Our teacher made us all get perfect scores or we had to take the test forever. The first time I took the test, I had answered that opera was when a fat lady with horns on her head sang really loud.

"Try," said my mother, getting cranky.

"I get the front on the way back," I said, still lying down.

"Fine," she said, "you get the front on the way home."

I sat up, but I shouldn't have. We had just pulled onto the highway. Right then, I looked out the window and saw some roadkill. You guessed it, it *had* been a bunny rabbit.

10

Booger was jabbering about how we still hadn't decorated the whole way to the mall.

My mom said, "I found the box of Easter decorations. I promise we'll do it tonight," then thought a second and added, "but do we have to?"

"I don't care," I said. I didn't.

"Yes, we do," said Booger.

He's such a little idiot.

"Let's just buy some candy," I suggested, "and put it around the house."

"And eat it and get sick," said my mother. "Well," she said, "we'll get a little candy, but we can't eat it until Easter. We're still in Lent."

I forgot to tell you we were in Lent, which is the six weeks before Easter and you're supposed to give up something. At our house you don't have to give up something, because it's already given up for you. My parents say we can't have dessert or candy during Lent. It makes me a tad cranky.

I wasn't telling my mom, but if we bought candy I was eating it, Lent or no Lent. Life was too short. I was going to enjoy it while I could and I was going to tell on Booger if I caught him even looking at candy.

We sat in the turn lane to the mall for what seemed like an hour. I wondered what would happen if our gas tank blew up.

"Where is our gas tank?" I asked my mom.

"I think it's under your seat," answered my mom, like it didn't matter. "Why do you ask?"

"Just wondering," I said.

I sat watching the cars go past and looking at the people waiting for our car to explode. A lady in a red convertible drove by.

"I'm going to get one of those," said Booger.

"Death on wheels," I just commented.

"Are not," said Booger.

"Yes they are," I said. "Think what happens to your stupid head when you roll the thing over in a wreck. Don't expect me to feel sorry for you."

My mother screamed, "I can't take it. Stop right now. Lizzie, I can't wait until you get out of this phase."

"What phase?" I asked.

"Whatever phase this is," she said.

Just then the light turned green, and since we were in front of the line and she wasn't moving like right that second, everyone started honking at her. I thought she was going to lose it. If she did lose it I thought she might have a major car accident. I decided to let it drop.

"Fine," I said, "I'm sorry for being alive."

"Just stay away from each other," she almost growled at us as she peeled out, "and try to be pleasant."

Talk about a phase, this thesis thing is really taking its toll on Mom. I can't wait till it's over. I think it's only a couple more months.

We actually found a parking place that didn't require a bus or a cab ride over to the mall.

"Nice work, Mom," I said sincerely.

"Don't be sarcastic," she shot back.

"I wasn't," I said.

She stopped a couple of cars with her arms extended like a crosswalk patrol person and we marched into the mall.

Inside the door was the guy or woman dressed as the Easter Bunny. You wouldn't think that was weird at all, would you? The weird part was that it had this little pink stuffed bunny that it practically pushed into my arms.

"Take it," the bunny said very matter-of-factly. I couldn't tell if it was a man with a high voice or a woman with a low voice. "You get a free bunny."

I tried to give it back. It probably had a bomb or drugs in it.

"I don't want one," I said.

"It's free," the person in the bunny disguise demanded, giving it back to me.

"I don't want it," I repeated, giving it back.

"It's a cute bunny," the big bunny said, "take it," and shoved it at me again.

"I don't want it," I said through gritted teeth, shoving it back at it pretty hard.

"You have to take it," the bunny person said forcefully, giving it back to me again.

I was ready to scream for my mother, the police, the FBI, and the ATF, who all had abandoned me. My mother was practically down the mall.

"No, I don't have to take anything," I yelled, giving it back again.

Booger stepped in front of me, taking the rabbit. "I'll take it," he said.

I said, "No you won't," and I tried to get it away from him.

Now my mother returned, realizing she'd left us behind.

"Mom," Booger whined, "the Easter Bunny wants to give me this bunny and she won't let me."

"He wants to give it to *me*," I said.

While we were talking, the Easter Bunny had turned and was running down the mall. Booger still had the pink bunny.

"Could we please just get inside even one store?" pleaded my mother.

"It's my bunny," said Booger.

"Who cares," I said.

I hated that bunny from the start. I didn't want it. I also would never trust anyone dressed up as a rabbit shoving things in people's faces.

The rabbit said it was for me, that I had to have it. That was confusing and a little more than frightening. The bunny probably really was a bomb and Booger was now going to blow up the mall. I looked at Booger holding onto the rabbit. For a second, I thought it winked at me. I told myself it was the lights.

Booger will lose it, I thought. I'll just stay away from him. Big deal.

He did almost lose it, too. I saw him set it down while we were in this one store that I knew didn't have girls' dresses but my mother had to check anyway. We even got all the way out of that store without him noticing that he'd dumped the bunny.

In another store my mother said, "Booker, why is this rabbit in my purse? It won't fit. You have to hang onto it."

"I didn't put it in your purse," said Booger.

"Don't look at me," I said, looking at them looking at me. "I'm starving to death," I added. "Do you know how many people die of hunger in a day?"

"No," said my mother, "and I don't want you to tell me. Can we try on just one dress before we think about eating?" my mother begged.

"Whatever," I said, "but if I faint, fall down, and get a concussion it isn't my fault."

"Oh, and I wouldn't dream of blaming you," she said, not even trying to be nice.

"I'm hungry, too," said Booger.

"This won't take long," said my mother, sighing. "Go sit down over there." She pointed to some chairs by the dressing rooms.

It didn't take long. It took forever and I mean truly forever before I even got into the dressing room. We couldn't agree on anything to even try on.

I kept saying, "I hate it" to everything she picked out — and I did. She only picked out retarded clothes that I wouldn't be caught dead wearing.

She finally gave in and asked me, "What don't you hate?"

I picked out a really cool dress. I went into the dressing room. I should have known she was tricking me. She was doing the old just-get-her-in-the-dressing-room-with-her-clothes-off-and-she'll-try-on-any-old-thing.

She came barging into my cubicle with her arms loaded. "Since you're in here," she said, "we'll just see how you look in these."

"I swear," I said, "I'm going to faint."

"Lizzie," she said like it was a dirty word and exited, probably to go get more.

I tried on five more ugly dresses after she told

me that the one I liked was too much money for a dress and then Booger opened the door so that the whole store saw me in my underwear. I almost started crying, I was so mad. I couldn't wait to get my hands on him. I couldn't believe they didn't have locks on the doors.

"Time for a break," said my mom, looking at her watch. "Oh no, how did it get so late? We have to get going."

"Fainting," I reminded.

"Lizzie." She ignored me. "How does your last year's dress fit?"

"The arms are tight," I answered.

"How tight?" she asked.

"Kind of tight — I don't know," I said. "I'm too hungry to remember."

"Okay, fine," she muttered, "let's go."

Booger was hanging out doing dumb things in front of the mirrors. I saw he'd left the bunny on the chair. When no one could see me, I grabbed it and threw it in the dressing room and shut the door.

"I'm ready," I said.

We walked down the mall. We got only a bagel for a snack. I wanted a cinnamon roll with extra frosting.

"It's too close to dinner, and it's Lent," said my mom.

"Candy," said Booger.

My mom stopped at the candy shop and bought

some jelly beans and some chocolate eggs wrapped in foil. They looked better than my bagel.

"We have to get home," said my mom. "I have so much to do."

We were heading to the parking lot. I worried about gang activity in the parking lot and whether our tires would be slashed.

"Where's my bunny?" whined Booger. "I lost my bunny."

"You're so irresponsible." I almost blew it and laughed.

"I'm sorry, Booker," my mother said, "I have to get home. We can't go look for it now. Your dad is going to church tonight and if I'm going to talk to him, we have to leave now."

"It serves you right," I wanted to say.

We got out to the car. I checked the tires and they were fine. I looked back at the mall, wondering when the bomb was set to go off.

"I get the front," I asserted.

"We know," my mother said impatiently.

"Look," said Booger, getting into the backseat. "Look what's here."

I didn't want to but I looked. Sitting in the back seat was the bunny.

"That's weird," said my mom.

"Get rid of it," I barked.

11

We got home just in time to make a quick dinner of spaghetti, with no meat of course, because my dad is still a vegetarian so we're all vegetarians. Booger is so stupid he says we're veterinarians. I tried to tell him that a veterinarian is an animal doctor and a vegetarian doesn't eat animals. He won't listen.

We basically only said "hi" to my dad. He did a quick check of what was happening and then we said "good-bye." He said he was being good and going to church. It was Maundy Thursday.

"Is there a Tuesday Wednesday?" asked Booger, which my mother thought was cute. How can she think a moron is cute? If I had said that she would have grounded me for two weeks.

"What is Maundy Thursday?" I asked, ignoring him.

"It's Maundy, not Monday," my mom said slowly to Booger like he was just learning to speak English, which he is, which is also more proof he's an alien. "Phil, why don't you tell them what it means."

Neither one of them knew for sure, but that didn't stop them from trying to fake it. They both did a couple of "I thinks" but they finally gave up and suggested we look it up in the dictionary. I did.

Guess what, the Maundy part means the foot-washing ceremony and Thursday means Thursday. Maundy Thursday is foot-washing ceremony Thursday.

I knew the priest washed feet on Maundy Thursday but I never knew that was why it was called that. I haven't been a ton of times to it, but when I went last year, I started laughing and I thought I was going to die trying not to laugh out loud.

I was laughing so hard inside I thought I was going to explode if I didn't let it out. I mean it was starting to come out my nose and ears. I could barely breathe. Everyone looked so silly running around barefoot. Someone knocked over the water and another lady had her feet washed with her pantyhose on. When that happened, I finally had to snort out my nose.

That is probably why they didn't ask me to go this year. It's weird. My dad says that's why he goes. He says it's unique and it busts up our ideas about what going to church is supposed to be.

My dad left and I helped clean up the dishes

without being asked, like a good girl. I didn't know what Booger was doing, and I didn't care. A couple of times I could hear him out in the living room. He sounded busy, whatever it was.

I was putting the pans away and my mom had left the kitchen. I had the funny feeling I was being watched. Do you ever get that feeling? Something in you knows that something else is looking at you. I turned around quickly and the door from the kitchen to the dining room was swinging ever so slightly.

I burst through it to yell at Booger to stop sneaking around. However, Booger wasn't in the dining room. No one was. Then I looked down at the floor.

There was that pink stupid bunny that was forced on us. I looked at it carefully and I thought I noticed it seemed a little different. It seemed fatter or something. I think it was a tad bigger. For a second I wondered if it was a different bunny, but it was the same ugly pink and had the same ribbon around its neck.

"You're bunny-nuts," I reminded myself. "You're getting jumpy about it. Lighten up."

I tried to take my own advice. I put the dish towel I was using down and walked into the living room like everything was safe and perfect in the world. I discovered why Booger had disappeared. He'd been decorating on his own.

It looked just lovely — in his dreams. He had

unpacked all the ugly worn-out stuff we'd collected forever. He also had that wonderful grass stuff strung from one end of the room to the other.

"Have you seen my bunny?" he asked.

"What bunny?" I said, knowing exactly which bunny he had lost again.

"The one they gave to me."

"They gave it to *me*," I said firmly.

"Well, it is mine now," he said.

"Go ahead. You can't keep track of it," I said.

"I can, too," he said. "It's right here."

He reached down and picked up the bunny. It was right at his feet. I could have sworn it wasn't there five seconds ago. I looked closely again to see if it was the bunny I saw in the dining room.

"Do you think it is fatter?" he asked me.

"Fatter than what?" I played dumb.

"Fatter," he explained, "because I think it is growing."

I could have said that I thought he was right, something was different about the bunny, but I was never going to agree with Booger on anything.

"Get your eyes checked," I said. "It's a stuffed bunny, they don't grow."

"I think this is a different kind of bunny," said Booger.

I got that weird pain in my head. I couldn't think for a minute, and then when I could think I couldn't remember what to think or how to ask him what he meant. My mom walked into the room.

"Oh, Booker," she said without any enthusiasm, "this is really nice."

He had little chickens and ducks on the TV. He had Easter baskets and all the five or six bunnies of several sizes we had, spread out around the room. He had put a ton of the fake grass on the coffee table, completely covering it. Then he had dumped the jelly beans we had bought in one big pile in the middle. I thought that was particularly attractive.

"What is that?" I asked, pointing to it.

Booger said, "It's a bunny nest."

"Oh," is all I said.

"Elizabeth, I think you better leave," said my mother.

"What have I done?" I asked.

"Nothing yet," she said, "but I know what's coming. Go do your homework."

I glared at both of them. I didn't have any homework. I grabbed the newspaper and a couple of catalogs and went to my room — but I didn't want to.

I left my room and bounced downstairs after a half an hour of reading about all the people who had been shot, bombed, hacked, abducted, mutilated, and attacked. I also looked at all the things I should buy in the catalogs. I put the paper and the catalogs back for a change. I usually forget to put them back on the buffet where we put the mail.

It's another thing that I do that drives my parents crazy. It isn't like they don't do things that drive me completely crazy. They get all bent because they think it's their paper and their mail. Just because they pay for the paper and the mail is addressed to them, they don't think they should be stored in my room. I don't think it's that big of a deal.

My mother had helped Booger redecorate. She'd moved some stuff and got rid of some stuff and completely dismantled the bunny nest. The jelly beans were now in a glass container.

I was kind of mad because I knew Booger had handled each one of them with his disgusting hands and I wasn't going to be able to eat them. I glanced around the room again and looked again at the jelly beans.

"Huh?" I said. "What is going on?"

I could swear the jelly beans had turned a different color. Before they were pastel pink, blue, green, yellow, and now they were pink. That's it, just pink.

"Mom?" I said quietly.

There was no answer. I walked over to the kitchen to see if she was there. She wasn't.

I walked back into the living room and jumped sixty-five feet in the air. The jelly beans were now all yellow.

12

The next day was Friday, Good Friday.
"If Jesus was crucified on Good Friday," I asked, "why would we call it good? Why wouldn't we call it Bad Friday?"

"Well . . . " said my mother, taking my toast out of our psycho toaster. It's truly psycho. You put bread in and you never know what or if it's coming out.

To get the bread in is the first major problem. You have to kind of bounce it in and out of the slots until the toaster decides to let it in. Then the toaster makes the decision, no matter what setting you put it on, to completely burn it, not toast it at all, or toast it perfectly.

Every time, which is practically every morning, my mother says, "I've got to buy a new toaster," but she never does. She says she's emotionally attached. It was a wedding present from someone she really cared about but I can't remember who.

My dad hates the toaster. He refuses to eat

toast, which is a good thing because he can never get the toaster to accept his bread. He can bounce bread in it like a basketball until his arm wears out and it won't go in. He told my mom that her emotional attachment was probably going to burn the house down one of these days.

I ate my toast and waited for my mother to answer my question, "Why is Good Friday good?"

"Well," my mother started again, "it's because it was a bad thing in one way but then you have Easter so it's a good thing. You can't have Easter without Good Friday. Does that make sense?"

"No," I said.

"You know what, Lizzie?" she asked, not really expecting an answer. "It's like this. Sometimes things don't make sense to us at the time and they seem like something bad, but then later you find out that the thing you thought was a bad thing was a really good thing. Sometimes you'll hear people say that getting cancer was the best thing that happened to them because it changed their lives completely. By fighting their disease they found out what was really important to them."

That sort of made sense by not making sense, or I was starting to completely not make any sense. Does that make sense?

"Okay," I said, "so like sometimes something bad is really good?"

"Exactly," she said.

"How do you know if something that happens

to you is really bad or if it's bad but it's going to be good?" I asked.

"You don't always know till much later," my mom replied. "Whoops, how do you feel about burnt toast? How about if I scrape it?" The toast she took out of the toaster was crispy black.

"I'll just skip it," I said. "I'll have some more cereal."

She then looked at the time.

"Make it fast," she said, "but chew. You're going to miss your bus."

I didn't miss my bus, but I almost did. It was at the stop and both Booger and I had to run. As long as you're running the bus driver will wait for you, but if you're walking you might as well turn around and go home.

At school there was no teacher in our room. Mrs. Rose was gone and there wasn't a sub there yet. In fact, the bell rang and there still wasn't a sub.

We all kind of sat there wondering if we were going to have a teacher or not. I was kind of into this fantasy of whether we could pull off not having a teacher and not have the rest of the school know. As long as we weren't loud and wild, we could probably get by.

I was starting to get into the idea when the door to our room burst open and a man came dashing in dressed in black with a top hat and a cape that was black on the outside and red on the inside. It was made of that shiny material that they use for wedding dresses.

He carried a cane and I think he had a fake handlebar mustache. He strode to the front of the class, took off his hat, and set it on Mrs. Rose's desk. He then pulled off his cape, and turned and wrote on the blackboard.

He wrote *Ralph*.

He turned to us and said, "Good morning, class. My name is Ralph and I'll be your magician this morning. Any questions?"

I had plenty. First being, was he a homicidal maniac with split personalities? Then, was he a kidnapper, or had he ever been convicted of a felony?

Julie asked, "Mr. Ralph, are you our substitute teacher?"

"Next question," he answered her, laughing.

I suddenly remembered that I knew this man and I didn't trust him. My memories of him came in flashes. This was the man we got our Christmas tree from. He was also the owner of the weird Halloween store. I was pretty sure this was the guy that sold us that weird turkey over the phone. This was the man that made me confused just to be around him. Was it him? Who was this guy?

If there was ever an alien abductee, he had to be it. Other kids tried to ask him questions and he wouldn't answer them either.

He'd say, "Ask something else," or "That's too easy, try a harder question."

I raised my hand.

"Elizabeth," he said, "what is your question?"

He threw me for a second because I was surprised that he knew my name.

I stuttered, "Who are you and why are you here?"

"Now class," he said, "that is a real question."

"Why am I here?" he pondered. "To everything there is a season, and a time to every purpose under heaven. I wonder what mine is? Who else wonders what their purpose is? Raise your hands, don't be shy."

No one raised their hands. They didn't know what he was talking about.

Juan said, "We're here because we have to be."

"Hmmmmm," said Ralph, moving his fingers like he was playing a piano.

I asked again, "Why are you here?"

"To teach," Ralph exclaimed loudly. He was obviously nuts. "To teach," he said, turning the hat on the desk over so the open part was facing upward, "and work a little magic."

He then reached into his pockets, pulled out white gloves, and put them on. He picked up the hat, tapping on the outside to show us it was solid. Then he punched his fist into it like a boxer, to prove that it was solid in there, too.

He set the hat back down on the desk, picked

up his cane, waved the cane across the hat, and then shoved his hand into the hat and pulled out a full-sized white rabbit. I swear to you, I don't know how he did it. It was like a real magic show. He pulled a real live bunny out of his hat in our classroom.

We couldn't help ourselves. It was cool. We clapped and cheered.

He said, "That's not all," and he started pulling more bunnies out of his hat.

He pulled about twelve out and we sat there with our mouths wide open like we were at the dentist. He stopped and we clapped again. We had a dozen bunnies and a crazy man in front of our class and we were clapping our hands off.

Bob, who sits in front of me, turned and said, "This is the best sub we've ever had."

I said, "He hasn't pulled an Uzi out of his hat yet."

Ralph, holding one of the bunnies up, said, "Elizabeth, have you ever seen this bunny before?"

"No," I said.

"You've seen quite a few, haven't you?"

I was immediately terrified. How did he know about my bunny thing? Why was he singling me out? I wanted to hide my head. He was looking at me very hard, like he was trying to see head lice from a distance of twenty feet.

He then shifted his focus and said, "Listen,

class, I have to tell you something."

He had one of the bunnies in his arms and was stroking it. The rest of the bunnies were moving around the classroom. The place smelled like alfalfa sprouts.

"I want to talk to you about rabbits. Actually, I want to talk to you about rabbit holes. To tell the truth, I don't know very much about rabbits but I know a lot about rabbit holes — not ordinary rabbit holes, mind you."

The class was silent. You could have heard a bunny wrinkling her nose.

"Are we going to say the Pledge of Allegiance?" interrupted Leah. Some people are so strange. They are like so into the rules.

"In due time," he said. "First, do any of you know the story of *Alice in Wonderland*?"

Most of us raised our hands.

"She was a young woman who went down a rabbit hole and ended up in a world that didn't make any sense to her. She thought everyone around her must be crazy and that she must be crazy, too, didn't she?"

We nodded yes.

"Life is often a mystery, isn't it? Things don't always make sense, do they? Well class, listen carefully, because rabbit holes are everywhere and you fall down them all the time."

He took a deep breath.

"Bam!" he blasted. "Something happens to you

and your life changes. Your surroundings no longer look familiar and there are strange people doing strange things — nothing makes sense — everything is crazy and, like Alice, all you want to do is go home and be safe. When you feel like that you know you've fallen down a rabbit hole."

"A real rabbit hole?" asked Matt.

"The most real," continued Ralph. "Your parents get divorced. Does that make sense? You're down a rabbit hole. You have a new brother or sister. It doesn't make sense. You're down a rabbit hole. You have to move to a new town and a new school. Nothing makes sense. You're down a rabbit hole. You grow up. Nothing makes sense. Everything is crazy and mixed up. You're down a rabbit hole."

I looked over at our door. Someone was obviously trying to get in but the door seemed to be locked. You could see the doorknob move. You couldn't see who it was because we'd turned our door window into a fake stained glass window with tissue paper, but you could hear them. Ralph was also looking at the door.

"Lizzie." He startled me by talking loud enough to drown out the sounds of the person trying to get in the door. "You can't help going down a rabbit hole and sometimes things just don't make sense."

Someone was knocking on the door.

"Class?" A woman's timid voice came from outside the door. "Could someone open the door, please?"

I stared at Ralph, wondering if we were hostages. He has putting on his cape.

"But," he continued, "listen carefully. You have a choice. You're down the rabbit hole and you get to choose. You can choose to live in fear or you can choose love. It's very simple.

"Now," he said, "if you would stand and say the Pledge of Allegiance."

Obediently but fully confused, we all stood and faced the flag by the door.

Just as we were saying, "I pledge allegiance to the flag . . . " the door popped open and in walked our sub, looking really flustered. She was young and new and no one knew her.

We stopped.

"That's all right," she said. "Continue."

We did, but no one was looking at the flag. We were snapping our heads around looking for Ralph. He had vanished.

You're right. It didn't make any sense. I wondered if we were down a rabbit hole.

13

At home, I checked the mailbox, which I usually don't do because you never know when you'll get a mail bomb. I guess I felt like living dangerously. Speaking of which, do you know why they don't have seat belts on school buses? Of all places, don't you think it makes sense to have people strapped in? I decided I would suggest that one to the principal.

I took the mail in the house, glancing at the jelly beans in the jar as I went by. They were bright red, all of them.

"Mom," I asked, "do you think I need counseling?"

"I swear I may not live through this phase. For what now?" she probed.

"I don't know," I said. "I was just wondering if I was crazy, like seeing things, if counseling would help."

"It depends on what you're seeing," she answered.

"Jelly beans, bunnies," I said.

"It's Easter," she said. "You're supposed to see those things."

"But they're everywhere," I stated, "and they change color."

"Is this a joke?" asked my mother. "I'm not getting it if it is."

"I think I'm down a rabbit hole," I explained.

"What?" she said, kind of surprised.

I started, "Sometimes the jelly beans are one color and then they're another and other than that the world is completely crazy."

She didn't get it.

"Of course they are," she said.

We stood in silence. I knew she wouldn't understand. No one understood. That's why it wasn't safe.

"Mom," I asked, "would you rather die by being crushed to death in an avalanche or would you rather drown in a flood?"

"Lizzie!" she screamed. "Enough. Don't be morbid."

"What's that?" I asked.

"Obsessed with death," she answered.

"I don't want to die," I said quietly.

She completely changed from crabby to nice.

"You won't, honey," she said softly. "Not for a very, very long time."

"How do you know?" I demanded.

"Mothers know," she said.

She came over and hugged me.

She then repeated, "Mothers know."

I felt safe for a while but then the news was on before dinner. There was an earthquake in China, a flood in California, a war somewhere, and a new outbreak of *Ebola* somewhere else. "Have a good evening," the anchorperson said at the end of the newscast.

We were having tofu lasagna for dinner. I was glad we were vegetarians. I heard there is at least some decrease in risk of getting *E. coli* if you're a vegetarian. Now if I didn't choke to death on dinner everything would be okay. I hoped everyone knew the Heimlich maneuver.

I tried to make polite conversation about what I'd recently read about the flesh-eating virus. It wasn't appreciated.

My mother said, "Elizabeth, this is neither the time nor the place."

"But I thought it was interesting," I said.

"It is," my mother said sternly, "but not at the dinner table."

"Well, what would you like to talk about?" I ventured.

"How was school today?" asked my dad.

"Okay," I said with my mouth full. I was really hungry.

Booger, who was only picking at his food, went on to give a complete rundown of his whole day at school.

He'd start up with, "And then we did . . . " this. "And then we did . . . " that. Finally he said, "and then we went home."

"Can I talk now?" I said after his fascinating life story. I wanted to tell them about Ralph.

"Sorry," my mom said. "We have to go. Tell it in the car."

"Go where?" said Booger.

"Church," said Dad.

"Why?" Booger questioned.

"It's Good Friday, stupid," I answered him.

"Lizzie!" exclaimed my mother. "Be nice to your brother. You know you love each other."

"That's a new approach," I wanted to say and of course didn't. *I'm* not stupid.

"It's Good Friday, Booker," my dad explained. "We have to go do the Stations of the Cross."

I was excited — just kidding. It was going to be an hour of going around the church following the cross, with people telling you about how Jesus died — minute by minute — talk about depressing.

I could have made a fuss and tried to stay home, but I didn't want to risk staying home alone. In the mail, my parents had gotten a notice that an ex-con had moved into the community.

"They make such nice neighbors," my dad had tried to joke.

My mother said to both Booger and myself, "Anyone who looks at you slightly funny, if you feel weird about anything, run and talk about it later."

"No kidding, Mom," I almost said. "There's nothing to worry about."

So I went to church. I was right. They talked about beatings and blood and suffering.

We got home and I went to bed and I had a nightmare. A big cat that smelled like medicine had abducted Booger and was driving him away. I caught up to him and tried to get him out of the car and the cat laughed at me. He drove away with Booger screaming for me to help him.

I woke up feeling horrible. I had to sleep the rest of the night with the light on. I hate that. I'm scared to have it dark — but if there is something bad out there, I also hate to have the light on so it can see me.

My mother looked at me in the morning and asked if I was coming down with something.

"Probably childhood leukemia," I stated.

"Lizzie, stop," she said.

"I didn't sleep good last night," I said.

"How come?" she asked.

"Bad dreams," I answered.

"Talk to your dad," she said.

My dad loves dreams. He loves everybody's dreams. His theory is that dreams are as important as what happens to us during the day. He thinks that sometimes they're even more important.

I couldn't find him to tell him. He had gone running and had probably been mowed down by an out-of-control garbage truck or attacked by a rabid dog. If not, he certainly was abducted for probably the thousandth time by a UFO.

"Let's dye eggs this morning," suggested my mom.

"Oh goody," said Booger.

I didn't say "Oh goody." I wouldn't be caught dead saying "Oh goody."

14

We only dyed a dozen eggs, six apiece. It hardly seemed worth all the mess and the smell. I swear those things start smelling the minute you boil water. I guess you either like eggs or you don't. I don't like them and I won't eat them.

"Can I eat one now?" asked Booger.

"I don't believe you," I said.

"Pass the salt please," replied Booger.

I held my nose while he ate a still-warm, hard-boiled egg that he had just dyed.

"What's the point of dyeing it?" I asked him with my nose still plugged.

"They taste better," he said with his mouth open and full of egg.

"Close your mouth. You are so disgusting."

My eggs looked good for a change. I kept them simple. I used only one or two colors. I didn't do what I did one year, which was to put each egg in every color. They ended up looking like some

93

strange swamp animal's eggs. Booger ate them anyway.

My mom was in a hurry. They were going out that night with friends and she had all these things she wanted to get done before then. I was going to have to stay home with Booger, which is my favorite thing to do on Saturday night. That, and waiting for serial killers to break down our door because they saw my parents leave.

Mom was trying to get everything ready for tomorrow today. I mean, she was ironing her dress and getting Booger's clothes ready. She was making some weird salad thing to take to my grandmother's house. It had cold canned beets in it. I wasn't eating it. She told me I'd better bring my dress to her now because she wasn't going to have time to iron it in the morning.

"Okay," I said, without listening to her.

Right then, I was listening to the news on the radio. A boat had tipped over and two men who were fishing were missing. Somewhere a bomb exploded, hurting nine people.

"Surprise," I wanted to scream, "the world isn't safe."

Booger and I started cleaning up the egg-dyeing mess. We were carrying the dye cups over to the sink. I got this great idea.

I talked Booger into letting me pour the blue and green dye over his hair in the sink. I told him it would make him look really cool. He believed me.

It didn't dye it much. It did make his ears kind of blue, though.

My mom came into the kitchen and lost it. "What are you doing?"

"Playing beauty parlor?" I tried.

She didn't think it was funny. I think my mother has lost her sense of humor.

"Why don't you try playing janitor and clean up this mess?" she scolded. "And I can't believe you did this to your brother's hair."

"He asked me to," I stated. Well, he sort of asked me to.

"I did not," said Booger, with his head still in the sink.

My mother was now rinsing his hair.

"Go get some shampoo and a towel," snapped my mother.

I couldn't believe she was getting so bent out of shape over a little hair dyeing. It wasn't even a little bit permanent. I went and got the shampoo and towel. Halfway down the stairs something tripped me.

I twisted my foot, which felt incredibly bad, and almost killed myself trying to keep from falling. I was okay, though. I turned to look at what had tripped me.

It was that maniac bunny lying on the stairs. I

kid you not. I think the bunny tripped me — on purpose. I kicked it down the stairs.

"I hope that hurts," I said down at it.

"Lizzie, hurry up," my mother yelled from the kitchen.

I ran in and handed her the stuff. She opened the shampoo and gave it to Booger.

"Scrub," she said.

Then she turned to me.

"Finish cleaning up the egg stuff and stay out of my way. I've got things to do and I don't need trouble."

"Of course," I said, kind of snotty like.

"Watch it," she said.

"Why are you so cranky?" I asked.

"I've got too much to do," she said. "I need help."

"Fine," I said. "What do you want me to do?"

"Stay out of trouble and don't make more work for me," she stated.

I cleaned up the newspapers we'd been dyeing the eggs on. You would not believe how ugly Booger's eggs were. They were definitely of the swamp variety. At least the time I did it, I did it on purpose.

Booger finished washing his hair and guess who got to go put the shampoo away. Heaving deep audible sighs, I took it and headed up the stairs. I was mad so it didn't register right away, but when I was at about the sixth stair, I remembered to look for the bunny. It wasn't there.

I tried not to think very hard about it. I figured someone had picked it up, like, I don't know, someone. I turned around and headed up the rest of the stairs.

At the top of the stairs I tripped again. This time I fell flat on my face.

"What the . . . ?" I said, looking down at where my feet were to see what had tripped me.

I saw the bunny's ears poking up above the stairs. I reached to grab them and the bunny jumped out of my reach down to the next step.

I stood up. My mind was jumbled. This didn't make sense. Stuffed animals without electronics or something don't move unless someone is moving them.

I set the shampoo down and reached down with both hands to the next step. The bunny anticipated my move and doing a high three-sixty, landed halfway down the flight of stairs. I obviously couldn't believe what I had just seen.

I felt like it wanted me to chase after it. It was like a dog who wanted you to play. I wasn't going to. I wasn't going to be crazy. I wasn't going to get in trouble. I wasn't going to have something weird happen to me. I was going to be safe and just do what I was told.

"Booger," I yelled, "come and get your stupid bunny."

15

I have to be honest with you. I mean I have been honest. I was not too thrilled about being left at home alone. I knew I wasn't going to be totally alone because I had Booger with me. Well, excuse me, but somehow that fact didn't give me a whole lot of peace of mind. I was mad at my parents because they didn't think it was all that dangerous.

I could think of five hundred things that could happen and almost made a list for them. On the other hand, I didn't want them to think I was a baby and that they needed to have a sitter over. I decided I'd just live with my fear one more time and keep the doors locked.

I asked myself, What could happen in two hours?

Booger and I ate vegetarian pizza while my parents were getting ready to go out. I was good and did the dishes. I told Booger he had to clean his own plate because I wasn't touching it, but he didn't.

"Fine," I said, and I let it sit in the sink.

My mom came into the kitchen and without even asking whose plate it was and why they hadn't cleaned it, washed it.

"Do not fight," said my dad. Then he said it again. "Do not fight, do you hear me?"

My mother added, "Please don't fight. We'll be gone for two hours. This is the number of the restaurant." She handed me the number on a piece of paper. "Call only if it is an emergency."

"If it's an emergency I'll dial nine-one-one," I said.

"That's fine." My dad laughed like it was funny. "Just call us, too."

It wasn't funny. It was serious. I was not going to mess around with emergencies. I watch TV. I've seen the shows with people breaking in while you're on the phone to 911. I know what to do.

"Don't be afraid," coached my mother. "You're perfectly safe. Lock the door behind us and put the answering machine on so you can screen the calls."

She said this like I wouldn't.

"Love you both," said my mom.

They left the house, and I turned to Booger.

"Do not," I said, "do not even think of giving me any trouble."

"You're not the mom," said Booger, "and you're not the boss of me."

I hate it when he does that.

"I get the TV in the living room," he said.

I wanted it but I said, "I don't even want to watch TV, so there."

I locked the doors, front and back. The answering machine was already on but I checked it anyway. I then went and checked all the windows and set up a slight booby trap by the door to the basement because I wasn't about to go down there and check it out.

The booby trap was two chairs with the recycling cans and glass on it in front of the door so anyone coming through would make a ton of noise moving them. To top it off I put the mop and the broom in an "X" behind the chairs. It didn't do anything extra but it looked good.

I went up to my room to hang out and wait for my parents to come home. I counted the steps going up to my room to make sure the number hadn't changed and I knew how much time I had when I heard a burglar come upstairs. I got my baseball bat out just in case I needed a weapon, and I set my alarm for two hours so I'd know when my parents should be home.

It was already getting dark outside. I had to turn on my light. I couldn't wait for summer when the days were longer.

I was lying down on my bed reading a book that

was overdue at the library. The house was quiet except for the muffled sounds of the TV that Booger was watching. I was pretty darn calm. I was prepared.

In fact, I was thinking I could go to sleep. I was kind of tired. Then, suddenly, I jerked myself to a sitting position.

What was that? I asked myself silently.

I heard running through the house. I heard the back door being unlocked and the door opening. Without thinking, I ran to my window to see if I could tell what was going on.

I saw Booger running really fast through our yard into the woods behind our house. We call them the woods but actually it's just some vacant lots that are overgrown with trees and bushes. I tried to get my window open to yell at him but by the time I fumbled around with the lock he was deep into the woods.

When I got it open, I yelled anyway, "Booger, you idiot. I'm telling Dad. You get back in here immediately if not sooner."

I sounded like my mother on that last part. Of course he didn't answer me. I stood at the window in complete panic. What was I supposed to do? It was getting darker fast.

I could look down and see that the back door was open.

"Oh, that's nice," I said. "That little moron didn't even close the door."

Then I wondered if the place was on fire. I figured that was why Booger had run away. The house was probably on fire and he just left me there to die of smoke inhalation. I wondered if I had time to wet a towel.

Then I figured there must be someone in the house. Maybe that was why Booger went running outside. I became petrified with fear.

I listened and listened by my door. I tried not to make any sound so I didn't give myself away. I couldn't hear anything except the TV.

I was going to pass out from not breathing. I finally took a breath, trying not to make any noise. I stood there.

Then I realized I had to do something. I couldn't sit there and wait for something bad to happen. I was going to have to get out of the house or die trying.

I thought about escaping out my window, but I left that as Plan B because I didn't want to jump from the porch roof down to the ground. You know how when you jump down from too high it makes your feet sting? That's what that jump does. I've done it before when I wasn't so afraid and I got in a huge amount of trouble.

"Courage," I told myself.

Myself answered, "Ha!"

I took a deep, deep breath, grabbed my baseball bat, and slowly opened the door. I peaked out. It was clear. I moved out and secured the hallway. It was still clear.

I looked down the stairs. There was nothing. I went down trying not to make the stairs squeak. One creaked and I stopped. I could hear the blood pounding in my ears. I waited. There was no sound.

I made my way down the rest of the stairs and into the living room. The room was empty. I turned the TV off. I figured we didn't need to waste electricity on top of everything. I moved through the lower half of the house, ready to club anything that moved.

I checked out the entire lower floor. The closets were the worst. I hate having to open them, knowing that something is going to pounce on you the minute you do.

The lower half of the house was clear. I went into the kitchen. The back door was wide open. I closed it. The booby trap in front of the basement door was still in place. I stood and listened carefully.

I thought I heard Booger's voice. He was calling me.

I was pretty sure I could hear him calling, "Lizzie, come here."

"No way," I said to myself.

Then I heard him again. I opened up the back door to see if I could hear better. It seemed like

I could hear him a little better. I was pretty sure it was him, although I did have the thought that it could be someone imitating Booger.

"What?" I screamed.

There was no answer.

"Booger?" I yelled. "Booger, where are you?"

I thought I heard a faint "Lizzie?"

"I'm just leaving him," I said to myself. "What is he doing out there anyway?"

Then I felt guilty. What if something was wrong? What if he was hurt and I didn't do anything? I wondered if I should dial 911 and get it over with.

Then I was mad at him for doing this to me. I hate making decisions like this. I got mad enough that I wasn't totally afraid.

"Fine," I said out loud. "I'll go get the little creep."

I grabbed my sweatshirt that was hanging by the back door.

Before closing the door I turned around and yelled, "Whoever is in here better be gone by the time I get back or you'll really be sorry, and I mean it."

I sounded tough.

16

I accidentally shut the door and heard it lock. I felt incredibly stupid. I was now locked out.

I said to myself, "What am I doing?" and then, "What am I going to do?"

I faintly heard Booger again. He didn't sound like he was in desperate trouble. I was mad at myself and him. It was like he was calling me to come look at something. He sounded like he was deep into the woods.

"There is only one thing you can do," I said to myself.

Well, there were other things I could have done. I should've gone and hid, or gone to the neighbors and called the police. However, I didn't think. No, for some reason, I decided I had to go find Booger by myself and then try to get back into the house.

I still had my baseball bat with me, but I decided it would be too heavy to drag around. I left it in the bushes. I thought I could always run and grab it if I needed it, which was totally ridiculous.

I headed to the woods. It was getting darker. The moon was rising.

I especially hate feeling afraid but still having to go ahead with doing what I'm afraid of anyway. I was already tired of pretending like I was courageous. I felt sorry for myself and wondered why no one ever came and rescued me.

Entering the woods, I thought I saw something stirring in the bushes ahead. I stopped dead in my tracks.

"Who's there?" I said timidly.

No one answered.

Then I thought I heard Booger again. The sound was coming from the lilac bushes over at the far side of the lot by the ditch. I headed toward them. He was sounding almost desperate, like maybe he really was hurt.

"Booger?" I whispered. "Booger? Is that you? Are you all right?"

Then a bird or a bat decided to take flight and dive-bomb me. I practically wet my pants. I tripped and got my leg hooked on a dead branch of a tree that was on the ground and tore my sweatpants.

I tried to remember what I was like before I got so afraid. I couldn't. I kept thinking that someone was going to jump out of the bushes and grab me any second. I felt super-stupid for not having a flashlight.

Then I saw something again. It was large. It

could have been Booger. Then I realized the ears were slightly bigger than Booger's.

"The rabbit?" I said out loud.

It turned and looked at me and then dove into the lilac bushes. Now let me tell you about these lilac bushes. They are very old, and we've made passages and tunnels through them. We are constantly playing games and pretending we live in them because from the outside they look like they are solid bushes but on the inside they can be a perfect place to hide.

I ran to the edge of the lilacs.

"Whoever you are," I said with as much force as I could, "I'm not coming in there after you, but I'm going to get my brother."

There was no sound coming from the lilac bushes.

"Booger," I said forcefully, "answer me."

Someone said, "Lizzie," as clear as a bell.

You know, it sounded like Booger but it didn't. Why didn't I question it more? Why didn't I go get help?

I went into the stupid bushes. I saw something moving up ahead, but I couldn't tell if it was the rabbit or Booger.

"Who are you?" I shouted.

No answer, and then I was mad. I got a surge of energy. I moved forward like a jungle fighter. I knew these lilacs like the back of my hand. You could call me Jungle Lizzie, Lord of the Lilacs.

The moon shone through a break in the branches and I saw the rabbit again. I moved quickly. I guess I thought I'd grab it just because. Call me Lilac Lizzie the Bunny Buster.

I grabbed it and immediately came to my senses. "What am I doing?" I cried.

Then I tried to let go. My hands were stuck to the fur like Velcro. As far as I could tell, I was permanently attached to the rabbit. The big stuffed bunny was alive, but it still felt like a stuffed bunny. It wasn't soft and warm like a real rabbit. It also didn't smell like an animal. It smelled like a stuffed bunny. It smelled like plastic and paper. It gave me the creeps.

Now that I was standing right next to it I realized it was at least my height. I started screaming. The bunny started moving. It was too strong. It was pulling me, dragging me. Then it took a dive into a hole.

That's right, folks. It dived into a hole with me on its back and I was falling down. I mean, we're talking straight down. Then I felt the bunny shrinking like someone had let the air out of a big balloon inside it. It shrank until it was a normal stuffed-bunny size and then it released its hold on my hands. All of a sudden I was alone, and I was falling fast. I'm trying to remember if I screamed. I must have but I don't remember.

I do remember it was pitch-black. At times, I couldn't tell if I was going down or up or sideways or anything. I was getting kind of airsick not being able to get my bearings. I fell and I fell and I fell.

I kept falling and then it felt like I was slowing down. Then I was almost floating more than I was falling. For a while, I thought maybe I'd landed, but when I slowly and carefully extended my arms I could feel the smooth, damp sides of the hole go slowly by. I was still moving downward.

I'm dying, I finally thought, and I'll have to wear the dress that is too tight in the arms for my funeral. I remembered that I forgot to have my mother iron it. I figured she'd be too upset that I was dead to iron it so I would be buried in a dress that was wrinkled and too tight in the arms.

I kept falling. I couldn't tell how long it was taking. It could have been seconds or minutes or hours. I kept falling like a snowflake. I then got the brainy idea that if I extended both my arms and legs at the same time, I could probably slow myself down until I stopped completely. I didn't even consider what I'd do if I did stop myself. Try to climb back out?

I slowly tried pressing my legs out first. Right off, my left foot hit a protruding rock. It was just enough force to throw me off. I practically broke my leg and banged against the opposite side of the hole with my whole body. I put my hands in front of my face to keep from breaking my nose as I ricocheted back over to the other side.

I wasn't going to try that again. I made sure I was still in one piece and I looked up. I could see the moon! Well, I could see what I thought was moonlight. The light looked like a single distant star, a pinhole in a black sky.

I was curiously calm. I wondered if this is what it felt like to jump out of an airplane. It wasn't so bad if it was. My only wish was for a parachute.

I was thinking about how I'd probably burn up as I passed the earth's core on my way to China. Then I actually laughed. I just thought it was funny, me in China trying to explain to my parents how I got there.

Then I noticed that I seemed to be slowing down even more. I could feel gusts of cool and warm air pushing up at me. I was slowing down big-time. In fact, I think I was hovering for a second, stopped in midair. Then I was lowered and my feet touched the ground and my body collapsed on top of them.

I was lying in a heap on the bottom of a very deep, very dark hole. To the best of my knowledge I was alive. I also thought I hadn't broken anything.

In the dark, I felt underneath me with my hands. I prayed not to touch a snake or whatever might live down there. I felt the touch of cold, smooth rock.

I yelled a weak, "Help," knowing there probably wasn't anyone to help me.

17

Then I heard a slow creak behind me, like a door opening. I turned, practically snapping my head off, and looked. There was light coming out of a doorway. The open, round-arched door was made of heavy wood like you'd see in a castle and the light was warm and bright, but any light would be in contrast to where I was standing.

At that point my mind was going fifty thousand miles an hour. I had it all figured out that it had been a plot. I decided I had been lured out of the house with Booger and I was being held hostage for ransom underground. How they wired the bunny I didn't know or care. Why they were picking on me I didn't know or care.

I knew this. I had to stay alive. I had to do whatever it took to survive until I could escape. I knew I had to keep a level head. I wondered if Booger was down the hole, too.

I also knew right then I had to make at least one decision. I could stay there in the dark where

I was and wait and see what would happen. That didn't feel right at all. I wanted to try to find Booger and plan an escape.

The door was standing there, open, like it was waiting for me. I thought that I could maybe go through that door and maybe face my captors. I thought that maybe it was a trap. Maybe there was a gorilla waiting inside the door ready to pounce on me. Then I thought that maybe there was somebody completely different from what I expected and that I'd find out that the whole thing was a joke and we'd have a good laugh.

I said to myself, "Lizzie, you're going to survive," and I didn't believe myself for one silly second.

I crawled over to the door because I didn't want to trip and fall. It was cold where I was but I could feel the warmth coming from the inside of the doorway. As I got up to it, I realized the doorway was only about four feet high. It was obviously designed for short people.

I peeked in. There wasn't any immediate sign of danger, captors, or Boogers. I made my move into the room.

I stood up against the wall. As far as I could tell, the long skinny room was empty of any people or animals. I was glad of that, although I could've used any friendly company right about then. I looked for signs that Booger had been in the room.

However, I didn't know what those signs might be. It wasn't like he was going to leave me a note.

The room was bright but there were no electric lights. It appeared to be lit only by candlelight. There were candles burning on shelves built into the walls. I could smell hot burning wax.

I looked up. The ceiling was so high up I could barely see it. I looked down the room. There was a roaring fire in a giant fireplace at the opposite end, providing lots of heat. The place was almost fancy-looking — for a cave.

It was like an underground banquet room or something. Down the center of the room was a long table with lots of lit candles on it. It was set for a feast.

It was going to be some party, too. Set out all the way down the table was the most delicious-looking food I'd ever seen. In fact, believe it or not, it was all my favorite foods. I bent over to breathe in the smell of the food. It smelled delicious. Like walking into a bakery attached to a really good restaurant — all sweet and spicy mixed up with the perfume of the flowers also on the table.

The food was hot. I could see steam rising off some of the dishes. Some had those warming candle things under them.

There were several kinds of pizza, all deep dish, which is my favorite. There was a huge fruit salad, and macaroni and cheese. There were doughnuts and homemade chocolate-chip cookies and banana cream pies and carrot cake.

There was a mountain of tortilla chips to make nachos, with really good-looking spicy melted cheese to pour on top of them. Next to that was a bowl of fresh salsa and another bowl of sour cream. I was suddenly starving to death. It must've been all the falling.

The table was set for at least thirty people, with fancy plates and a million pieces of silverware. It was like in a restaurant where you don't know which fork to use. There were place cards at each plate. I picked one up.

It said "Lizzie."

It totally freaked me out.

I grabbed the next one. It said "Elizabeth."

I almost choked. I ran from one place to the next. Each card had my name on it, or a form of my name. Sometimes they said "Lizzie" and some-times "Elizabeth" and other times "Liz," but it was my name every time.

I was trying to put the whole thing together. I thought about the rabbit. I thought about how I got there. I thought about who would know I was coming. I was wondering what I was supposed to do.

I tried again to get my facts straight. I'd fallen down a rabbit hole, attached to a stuffed bunny. I was probably kidnapped. My parents were probably getting the ransom call right now. I was in a hall with dinner laid out. I was the only guest. Okay, I admit it, nothing made sense.

Then I head a whisper. I thought it was inside the walls or something but then I realized that it was coming from inside me.

It reminded me, "When you fall down a rabbit hole, things don't make sense."

"All right, it may not make sense, but I'm starved."

I sat myself down at the table and put the cloth napkin on my lap. I thought that would've made my mother happy. I loaded up my plate with the chips and cheese, and heaped salsa and sour cream on them, and it looked quite tasty.

Then my inside voice whispered one word: "Persephone."

A little shock went through my body.

I said it out loud. "Persephone?"

A wind blew through the room like a window had just been opened. I could feel it go through my skin like I wasn't even there. The candles flickered. Some of the place cards blew off the table. I felt cold. Deep inside my body, I felt like something was trying to push the thought of Persephone out of my brain.

I'm here to tell you, they can do a lot of things to you, but no one is going to tell me what to think. I started repeating "Persephone, Persephone, Persephone . . . " first quietly and then out loud, till I was finally screaming it.

Suddenly I knew what it was about Persephone that I needed to remember.

"I'm not eating," I said.

Persephone ate that one dang pomegranate underground and ended up Queen of the Dead. I could just imagine what eating a whole plate of underground nachos would get you. The wind stopped. There was a rumble and the table shook. I heard the clank of the prisms hanging from the candle holders on the table. They were swaying.

In front of me the once-delicious food was moving. At least at first I thought it was just moving, but then I realized it was transforming. The food was dissolving into dust. I was just sick watching it go. I jumped sixty-five feet because I saw a rat run out of what used to be the carrot cake.

The room suddenly smelled like hot dirty feet. It wasn't me. I heard a pounding coming from the end of the room where I had entered. It sounded like a very slow jackhammer. The door was now shut.

The candles were going out one by one, like a ghost was blowing them out. I slammed my chair away from the table and pressed myself against the stone wall behind me. It was getting dark in the room.

I ran to the opposite end of the room, by the fireplace. There looked like there was a doorknob next to the fire, which also seemed to be dying

116

out. Then I did something totally stupid. Talk about not making sense. I stopped.

I stopped to look closely at the carvings around the fireplace, like I was in a museum. The carvings were of rabbits. There were all these cute bunnies and they were dancing under the moon. There was a full moon over one group and then a quarter moon over another and a half moon over still another group. All the phases of the moon were covered, waxing and waning to beat the band.

Meanwhile the candles were going out and the pounding was getting louder and coming toward me. It was like it was driving me out of the room.

"Why? Why? Why?" I wanted to ask. "Why is this happening to me?"

I grabbed the doorknob just before the last candle and the fire went completely out. I know you'll think I'm stupid, but I knocked on the door first. I didn't think this was the time to be ill-mannered. I hoped with all my heart that Booger was on the other side and would open the door.

No one answered. The pounding stopped. The room was dark except for the light from the fireplace and it was going out, too. I thought I could hear someone breathing in the room.

"Don't think about it," I told myself, so of course it was all I thought about. I quickly opened the door, stepped out, and slammed it shut behind me.

18

I thought my back was against the door, but I could no longer feel it supporting me. It took a minute for my eyes to adjust to the new light. I could still hear pounding, but it sounded different. Then I realized it was my own pounding heartbeat I was hearing. It sounded like racehorse hooves.

I felt not only afraid but extremely lonely. I wanted anyone to be here with me. I wondered if I'd ever see anyone again.

My eyes were adjusting. I was outside. Yes, I know it didn't make sense. It was still night and I seemed to be in like a treeless, bushless, grassless desert. There were a million bright stars in the sky.

Man, the moon is bright, I thought, looking up.

Get ready. It wasn't the moon that was bright. Unless the moon is blue.

I was looking up or down, take your pick, at Earth. I knew it was Earth. It was just like it looked in the pictures from space. I have a poster of it on my wall that says, "Love your mother."

To say I was totally freaking out is to put it mildly. My whole body was shaking.

"I'm not on Earth?" I kept asking someone, I guess myself.

Nothing made sense. Nothing at all. How could I be inside the earth and yet not on it? Did I fall up instead of down? Was I kidnapped or not? I had a ton more questions than answers.

I glanced at my surroundings. The door was gone. I didn't have a clue where it went. I hadn't moved. It must've. I was all alone, standing in the middle of what looked suspiciously like a — I didn't believe it — crater. I was really really really on the moon.

I was not only on the moon, but I was on the moon without a spacesuit, breathing like there was no tomorrow, which, at that point, there probably wasn't.

I said to myself, "Lizzie, get real, you're not on the moon. You're breathing. There is no atmosphere on the moon. If you're on the moon you must be . . ."

I couldn't say it even to myself. The word was "dead." I couldn't believe it. My mind was swimming. I didn't want to be dead. And I most certainly didn't want to be dead *and* on the moon.

Is this where you go when you die? I wondered. The moon is heaven?

That made me kind of laugh. Then I looked at the earth and I started crying. I mean I was all of a sudden crying my stupid eyes out. My nose was running like a fire hose and I didn't have anything to wipe it with except my sleeve. I was dead and I missed everyone. I wanted to go home. I didn't want to be stuck on the moon.

The door, I thought, still crying. Maybe I could find it and go back through the door?

However, I couldn't find it. I was running around the crater kicking up moon dust like a lunatic. There was no hint of a door and I realized, climbing up the side of the crater, that the moon is a very big place.

I sat on a large moon rock. I calmed myself down slightly by deep breathing. For some completely idiotic reason I decided right then to wonder how close I was to where the astronauts landed. Thinking about the astronauts, I reached down, picked up a small moon rock, and put it in my pocket.

I wondered if anyone could see me with a telescope. Maybe they'd come get me. I waved my arms at them. Then I remembered I might be dead and they couldn't see me, and I started crying again. Then I stopped. I was too afraid to cry.

I figured if I was dead, then there should be other dead people around. There are worse things than being alone, and I had the icky feeling that I wasn't. I didn't know who else was on the moon.

I certainly didn't want to find out, especially if it was like a cannibal alien or something. I was scaring myself silly.

I asked myself, "How can you be afraid if you're dead? If you're already dead, no one can kill you."

I didn't have an answer. I sat. I cried some more. I was afraid.

I finally looked up at the earth so I could feel even worse knowing everyone I knew was up there and I was stuck on the moon. I noticed something really cool. From the moon, the earth looked only beautiful and friendly. It glowed so warmly, all blue and green with swirling white clouds, that I couldn't believe anything could be bad there. I couldn't believe that I was ever afraid there. I was really getting into this feeling.

Then there was this thing, this black kind of cloud off to the left of the earth. It was moving. It was slowly moving toward the earth.

"It's going to eat the earth," I said out loud.

The black thing was getting darker, and it was whirling. It was like a giant round black tornado — rabbit hole!

"It's a stupid black rabbit hole!" I screamed without thinking.

No sooner had I said that than the hole jumped itself right over next to the earth. Then, as I watched in horror and disbelief, the entire earth was simply and quickly sucked down that black rabbit hole like it was going down a drain. Without any warning to anyone, just like that — bam! — it was gone. My world was gone, no longer there, vanished, disappeared, whatever.

I just stood there totally dumb and numb. I was frozen with confusion. My mind wouldn't and couldn't comprehend what my eyes had just witnessed.

Then I realized the black thing was coming toward the moon. I had this totally bizarre thought that I was almost drawing it toward me. I didn't know how I was doing it, so I couldn't stop.

I remembered the door — I had to find the door. I thought maybe it might be on the ground. Well, anything was possible. I started kicking away some of the moon dust or dirt, whatever you call it. I hit something solid and flat. I got down on my hands and knees. It was like a tombstone. I brushed away the dirt from it.

It said, FEAR OR LOVE, THE CHOICE IS YOURS.

"If that's the choice," I said as loud as I could to whoever could possibly hear me, "I choose love."

The black rabbit hole was getting closer.

This is it, I thought, looking up at it and then putting my head in my hands.

"Please, pretty please, get me out of here," I prayed, digging my hands into the moon dust trying to find something to hang onto.

Then I thought I heard a familiar voice.

"Lizzie!" it yelled.

"Booger," I screamed, all excited, "where are you?"

I couldn't see him. I could barely hear him. The black rabbit hole thing was all around me. There was moon dust flying everywhere.

"Right here," he said. "Give me your hand."

"Where?" I cried. I was beyond desperate. I wanted to find him so bad. I wanted to hang onto Booger's hand with all my might.

"Here," he said clear as a bell, "right here. Grab on."

I crawled, reaching out toward the sound of his voice. I felt a hole in the ground. I stuck my hand in it and felt Booger's hand. It was his for sure. It was grubby as ever.

I wanted to say, "Do you ever wash these things?" but I didn't. I was so happy to touch him. I felt really stupid. At that moment, I wanted to tell Booger that I loved him. I guess that's the final proof that I was crazy.

"Hang on!" he yelled.

I hung on with everything I had and closed my eyes. I felt like I was in the center of the tornado, being ripped apart. I felt Booger pulling on my arm like he was pulling it off.

I wanted to say, "Don't pull so hard," but then he gave a huge jerk and I felt myself bump on the ground. The roar of the black rabbit hole had stopped. I slowly opened my eyes.

19

My eyes were wide open. I was still outside and it looked like, well, looked very much like Earth. I looked up. The moon was up where it was supposed to be.

"Booger?" I said.

"What?" he said.

"Is that you?"

"No, it's the Easter Bunny," he said.

"Not funny," I said.

Then I did one of the strange things that I've only done a couple of times in my life. I hugged him.

"Get off me," he said.

"I'm alive!" I yelled.

"Ya, so what?" said Booger.

"You saved my life," I said.

"I did?"

I said, "Let's get back to the house."

"Okay," he said as we got up. "What were you doing out here anyway?"

"I went after you," I said.

"Wrong," he said. "I was in the house and saw you leave and I went after you."

"Huh?" I said.

We ran through the rest of the woods and across our backyard. In an instant we were standing on our back porch.

"Wait," I said, "I have to get my baseball bat." I tried to pick it up from where I thought I left it. It wasn't there.

"Why would it be there?" said Booger.

"Because I put it there," I snapped. "Did you move it?"

"It's probably up in your room. You won't even let me touch it."

I stared him down.

"Did I really save your life?" asked Booger.

I went toward the door.

"Dang," I said, "I forgot. I locked us out."

"What are you talking about?" he said, puzzled. He reached past me, opened the back door, and walked into the house.

"It was locked," I said, "and I'm not lying."

He turned to me. "What were you doing in that hole in the bushes? Were you hiding from someone? You acted like you couldn't get out."

It was like a water balloon broke inside me. Everything came gushing out.

"I was in a hole all right." I started crying. "Do you realize that I was on the moon and I was totally afraid and I thought I was kidnapped and then I thought I was dead and then this big black thing was after me and then you gave me your hand . . . "

"You're nuts," said Booger.

"I'll prove it," I said.

I reached into my pocket to find my moon rock. I was ecstatic. It was there. I took it out and laid it on the kitchen counter.

"What's that?" Booger asked, completely baffled by my actions.

"It happens to be a moon rock," I answered smugly.

"It just looks like a plain old rock to me," he said.

It was a shock, but I realized he was right. It looked like a normal rock.

"Well," I stated firmly, "it isn't. It's a rock from the moon."

"Prove it," he dared.

I stood there. I couldn't prove it. How could I prove it?

"Well . . . well . . . well . . . " I sputtered, "if you're too stupid to tell whether it's a moon rock or not, I certainly can't help you."

"It's not a moon rock," he said, walking away from me into the living room.

Total confusion hit me.

"What is going on?" I said out loud.

I looked down at my sweatpants. Where there

should've been a big hole where I ripped them, they were as good as new.

I followed Booger into the living room.

"You mean," I said, "you weren't outside chasing the rabbit?"

"What rabbit?" asked Booger. "Are you trying to confuse me? Are you playing a trick on me? Is this like an April Fool's thing?"

"You," I said calmly, "went outside . . . I think, to chase the bunny, and I went after you to save you. You were calling me."

"No I wasn't," he said. "I heard you go out the back door and I followed you. You went into the lilacs and I came and pulled you out of that hole."

I could've just thrown up. I was totally confused. Nothing, absolutely nothing made any sense. I went over and ate a handful of jelly beans that were all different colors, just the way we bought them.

Right then my parents walked in the door.

"Hi, kids," said my mom. "How did it go?"

Booger looked at me and then said, "Fine. I saved Lizzie's life."

My mom was completely alarmed.

"What?" she screamed.

"He's just kidding," I lied. "We were playing a game."

She calmed down. I know I shouldn't have lied but I didn't know how to explain it. I didn't know what it all meant. I'd tell her the truth later and apologize for lying, but not in front of Booger, who would change the whole story.

My dad said, "Lizzie, you really shouldn't eat a bunch of sugar before bedtime."

When he said the word "bedtime," I realized I was exhausted. I guess being crazy makes you tired.

"Good night," I said. "I'm totally whipped."

"Well, good for you," said my dad. "I like it when you take care of yourself. Go to bed when you're tired."

My mom said, "I hope you're not getting sick?"

"Me, too," I said.

I went upstairs like a zombie on a mission. I brushed my teeth, washed my face, went into my room, and put on my nightgown. Without even thinking about it, I went over to my window, unlocked it, opened it up, left it unlocked, and got into bed. From my bed I could see that my bat was against the wall where I usually keep it.

I quickly went to sleep. I was confused and nothing made any sense at all, but I wasn't afraid anymore.

20

I woke up the next morning. It was a beautiful day. It was a perfect day. I felt so different. It was like a fog had lifted.

I couldn't quite figure out what it was, and then I knew. I didn't feel afraid. I wasn't feeling like someone was going to get me. I jumped out of my bed and looked out my window.

The birds were singing. I don't know how else to describe it, but to say that the world looked new. It looked safe and fresh and innocent.

Then I remembered it was Easter Sunday. I got out my dress. It wasn't too wrinkled. I put it on — tight as anything in the arms. They were probably going to fall asleep and I didn't care.

I went downstairs in my good shoes, which I normally hate, but today I didn't even mind them.

"Happy Easter," said my mom, adding, "Oh my, the arms are a little tight."

"They're okay," I said. "I'll wear a sweater."

She looked at me, shocked. I guess she was expecting a fight.

"The Easter Bunny left you a present," she said with a big grin.

I must've looked different. I was a little apprehensive of what that statement actually meant.

"Are you okay, Lizzie?" she said, handing me a basket full of candy.

"Oh, *that* Easter Bunny," I said, laughing.

"Don't eat it all now," she said. "Booker has already gone through half of his without me knowing it and he'll probably be sick in church."

I could've said something nasty, but I didn't. I felt too good. Nothing could ruin this day.

We ate breakfast and went to church. I didn't fight with Booger on the way there. I was too busy looking out the window at how great spring was. You know what? I didn't see any rabbits.

Church was even okay. We started out and ended it by saying "Alleluia," and we sang it all over the place. I sang my heart out.

The priest said that Easter was the death of fear. On the way up to Communion, Booger tripped and fell flat and I even helped him up. I practically ripped my dress because my sleeves were so tight, but I helped him up.

After church we got in the car to go to my grandmother's, where I'd probably have to hunt Easter eggs even though I'm too old. Surprise! I didn't care.

"I like Easter," said my dad. "It's so . . . well . . . alive."

"Me, too," I said, and then I added, "Alleluia," at the top of my lungs.

Everyone, including my dad, who should've had his eyes on the road, turned and looked at me like I was nuts.

I didn't care. I started laughing, and so did they.

Hi. This is Booker. It's true. Lizzie is crazy and I did save her life and my name is Booker not Booger.

Booker

APPLE®PAPERBACKS

Pick an Apple and Polish Off Some Great Reading!

BEST-SELLING APPLE TITLES

- ☐ MT43944-8 **Afternoon of the Elves** Janet Taylor Lisle $2.99
- ☐ MT41624-3 **The Captive** Joyce Hansen $3.50
- ☐ MT43266-4 **Circle of Gold** Candy Dawson Boyd $3.50
- ☐ MT44064-0 **Class President** Johanna Hurwitz $2.75
- ☐ MT45436-6 **Cousins** Virginia Hamilton $2.95
- ☐ MT43130-7 **The Forgotten Door** Alexander Key $2.95
- ☐ MT44569-3 **Freedom Crossing** Margaret Goff Clark $2.95
- ☐ MT44036-5 **George Washington's Socks**
  Elvira Woodruff $2.95
- ☐ MT41708-8 **The Secret of NIMH** Robert C. O'Brien $2.75
- ☐ MT42537-4 **Snow Treasure** Marie McSwigan $2.95
- ☐ MT46921-5 **Steal Away** Jennifer Armstrong $3.50

Available wherever you buy books, or use this order form.

- -

SCHOLASTIC INC.
Box 7502, 2931 East McCarty Street, Jefferson City, MO 65102

Please send me the books I have checked above. I am enclosing $ _____ (please add $2.00 to cover shipping and handling). Send check or money order—no cash or C.O.D.s please.

Name_____Birth Date_____

Address_____

City_____State/Zip_____

Please allow four to six weeks for delivery. Offer good in the U.S.A. only. Sorry, mail orders are not available to residents of Canada. Prices subject to change.

GET
Goosebumps®
by R.L. Stine

☐ BAB45365-3	#1	Welcome to Dead House	$3.99
☐ BAB45369-6	#5	The Curse of the Mummy's Tomb	$3.99
☐ BAB49445-7	#10	The Ghost Next Door	$3.99
☐ BAB49450-3	#15	You Can't Scare Me!	$3.99
☐ BAB47742-0	#20	The Scarecrow Walks at Midnight	$3.99
☐ BAB48355-2	#25	Attack of the Mutant	$3.99
☐ BAB48350-1	#26	My Hairiest Adventure	$3.99
☐ BAB48351-X	#27	A Night in Terror Tower	$3.99
☐ BAB48352-8	#28	The Cuckoo Clock of Doom	$3.99
☐ BAB48347-1	#29	Monster Blood III	$3.99
☐ BAB48348-X	#30	It Came from Beneath the Sink	$3.99
☐ BAB48349-8	#31	The Night of the Living Dummy II	$3.99
☐ BAB48344-7	#32	The Barking Ghost	$3.99
☐ BAB48345-5	#33	The Horror at Camp Jellyjam	$3.99
☐ BAB48346-3	#34	Revenge of the Lawn Gnomes	$3.99
☐ BAB48340-4	#35	A Shocker on Shock Street	$3.99
☐ BAB56873-6	#36	The Haunted Mask II	$3.99
☐ BAB56874-4	#37	The Headless Ghost	$3.99
☐ BAB56875-2	#38	The Abominable Snowman of Pasadena	$3.99
☐ BAB56676-0	#39	How I Got My Shrunken Head	$3.99
☐ BAB56877-9	#40	Night of the Living Dummy III	$3.99
☐ BAB56878-7	#41	Bad Hare Day	$3.99
☐ BAB56879-5	#42	Egg Monsters from Mars	$3.99

Scare me, thrill me, mail me GOOSEBUMPS Now!